GH00731277

A Hake's Tail

A Psychedelic Tale of Apathy

Lester Louis Gartland

Don't bend; don't water it down; don't try to make it logical; don't edit your own soul according to the fashion. Rather, follow your most intense obsessions mercilessly. Only if you do that can you hope to make the reader feel a particle of what you, the writer, have known and feel compelled to share."

- Anne Rice
(On Franz Kafka, 1995)

For Paul Gartland and Ed Matthews.

PROLOGUE

"Oh, for goodness' sake, Frank. Don't be so squeamish, it looks like a nice piece of fish. The waiters are looking at us... I'm getting embarrassed, eat a bit would you!"

Three waiters stood by the floor-to-ceiling windows which looked out to a moonlit Lisbon beach. They stood there ruffling their white blazers and observing the odd couple who were laughing at the only booked table in the restaurant. Sarah, for the waiters' sake, attempted to look nonchalant and took a sip from her glass of vinho verde. Her less than stellar performance was quickly ruined however when she corpsed and snorted with laughter at the way her husband poked and prodded at his *authentic Portuguese meal*. In a jolt she brought her hand up to cover her mouth. Some wine expelled from her nostrils and spattered into her palm before it rolled off her fingers and pattered onto the white linen tablecloth, narrowly missing the *bloody endless* rows of silverware which made her plate look like a *maths equation*. Seeing this, Frank quickly diverted any attention away from him by *grassing her up* to the restaurant staff as he announced:

"Careful, love! You almost put out the candle doing that!"

"Stop it, Frank! It's your bloody fault anyway, Ahab. Sitting across from me staring at that whale on your plate."

Frank giggled like a schoolboy as he picked up his fork, *I think I'm using the right one*, and manipulated the pescadilla de rosca on his plate. *I knew I should have got the steak, always play it safe when you're on holiday.* The fish's scales were baked into it, and the whole thing had gone brown and *angry.* What remained of its fins had crusted into thick twiggy hairs covering its body, and it was displayed on the plate in a complete circle, its own needle-like teeth clamping down on its tail, devouring itself like an ouroboros.

"It's like a fucking sea monster, Sarah! Look at it! It's staring at me. It's going to finish eating itself then it's going to move onto me!"

"Stop making me laugh, Frank, you'll ruin my makeup."

"I wish this thing had some makeup."

"I said stop it! Try a bit for the love of God, the waiters are looking at us... Oh! Shh shh, one's coming over – shut up... Yes, no everything's lovely thank you, oh and the wine is fantastic... oh, you don't have to – it's just a little bit on the tablecloth, sorry. Oh-bree-gardo Sen-yor... Come on, Frank, eat a bit."

Frank stared the hake down for a few seconds and took a deep breath in. His culinary courage waxed, *might as well, cost me enough*, his knife pushed into the *pes-ka-dee-oh's* crispy skin and layers of it crumbled off. *Oh, yeah... lovely... a fish croissant.* He withdrew his knife, *I hope I'm using the right one*, and removed his gold wristwatch.

"Right, no time like the present, ey love?"

His fork depressed into the fish's crispy back which, in turn, forced its head to raise towards Frank. The tail flopped out of its dry serrated teeth and as soon as Frank took a bite, everything but the table went black. No Mediterranean waves crashing in the background, no 'authentic' music, no waiters... and no Sarah. Black.

Frank closed the photo album and placed it on the bedside cabinet.

"Good times."

He sighed as his *fat old arse* compressed the mattress to its limit, rotated onto his side and tucked himself in. Artemis was already at the foot of the bed, *hogging the mattress and getting fur all over the place.*

"Nun-night, girl."

1

At first, Frank felt wary by how tranquil everything was. He made a genuine effort not to cause too much disturbance to the mattress as he gently sat up in his bed and noticed that the usual noise of refuse disposal trucks and early commuters - which would normally be bleeding through the single-glazed window - was absent. Curiouser still, the neighbours weren't arguing or playing obnoxious *bloody awful four-to-the-floor 'music'* in a drunken stupor as they usually would either. Nor was their *yappy little rat* barking in the back garden. He sat fully upright on the side of the bed and his bare feet dangled in the pale sunlight which tentatively glowed through the thin curtains, *blackout fibres my arse*. Frank looked over his shoulder and saw Sarah still sleeping peacefully. She hadn't been disturbed by Frank waking up as she often would have. Usually, Sarah would have woken up at the sound of Frank's mid-nightmare gasps and - through half closed eyes - she would place a palm on his sweaty forehead and proceed to question him about the subject of his bad dream, which was most often the moon.

"No noises, no bad dreams... well what woke me then?"

Frank thought on this for a while as he stretched out his old, creaking back, then – as he had come up with no answer - decided to go for a walk around the neighbourhood, *a red-eye patrol,* while the rest of it still slept.

The sunrise was beautiful. Pinks and peaches bordered what few clouds there were. The rays were just the right temperature on his forearms, which Frank had willingly exposed by pushing up the sleeves of his striped pyjamas. When he closed his eyes, the backs of his eyelids glowed a wonderful citrus colour. His nostrils filled with grass and pine and morning dew. It reminded him of the curious perfume he once gifted to his wife, which she wore politely, one time. The vision of Sarah still sleeping peacefully in their bed entered his mind. As it did, Frank felt the most overwhelming urge to return to her.

"Shouldn't really leave her in the house alone at this hour, heaven only knows who could decide to just let themselves in."
He sharply turned back on himself to rendezvous with his wife but as he did – and just as hastily as his pivot – the sun set, and night had returned. It was dark and cold now, and Frank couldn't make out anything for a minute or so before, one by one, with a time-keepers rhythm, the streetlights turned on, each one with a loud bang. The first startled Frank the most as it popped and zapped directly above him, then the lights which followed dictated the path ahead. Frank passed under the amber glow of the streetlights; they

added a pulsating copper lustre to the asphalt which sprawled out to his left.

"Not a car in sight."

He stuffed his hands into the pockets of his overcoat, he could feel the cold begin to cease up the fine motor skills in his ageing and aching hands and he needed warmth to regain control of them. Although Frank had not noticed any looming danger in his surroundings, he had always been the type who held a romanticised notion of what it meant to be a combatant in modern days. The delusions of his own capabilities and robustness let Frank fancy himself as a decorated warrior of a dying breed. Of course, there was rarely need for confrontational physicality in his life, but Frank always found something appealing in the idea of *digging deep into the darkness within him, pulling it to the surface, and utilising it as a rudimentary tool for good & justice*, or honour... or even revenge depending on how Frank woke up on the given day - and what genre of movie he had watched the previous night, *Ben Hur last night, late to bed again*. He had been known to get carried away with these delusions of heroism in his younger years, but now he was older and wiser he made a significant attempt to be in control of his moral reasoning, especially as now he knew what it cost to let his emotions take the wheel and his sins ride the gas.

The soles of his feet rubbed inside his old in-need-of-replacing slippers. *Not really designed for walking,* he thought. The rows of trees to his right had cleared, the thick smog of leaves gave way for a turn in the road which led to a suburban close that boasted lawns, garages, mailboxes, fences, *the Stepford works*. As Frank turned up into the quaint suburban labyrinth, he heard the popping and zapping again as darkness returned. Something had killed all the streetlights. All was black, no more copper lustre, no longer the comforting faint buzzing of utility. All that was left were dark silhouettes of houses, silent and still, *leering*. And there was Frank, stopped in his tracks, frantically forming and unforming his fists in his pockets, listening for any sudden rustling, quick footsteps, shallow breathing, *safeties being turned off, hammers being slowly pulled back.* All this happened within seconds, but it was long enough for beads of sweat to form on Frank's upper lip – they may have been hidden by his charcoaled moustache, but Frank's eyes told the whole story. Shortly after, he noticed more beads forming on his forehead, but this wasn't from anticipation, this flop sweat was from the change in temperature. He could feel an intense heat beating down on him with great ferocity, and beams of light now speared through the clouds and splashed over the lawns, garages et al. *Off on, off on* he thought. The sun illuminated everything with such unbearable brilliance he began to long for the known uncertainty of the darkness. Attempting to adjust from the rapid changes of light, to dark, and back again *with bells on*, Frank's eyes could only open enough for half a squint, and his hands made their way from his pockets to reach out in front of himself, *like a scooby doo villain,* he stumbled toward the first house on the street.

"Can't see a bloody thing! What the hell is going on? Some sort of... reverse eclipse, I imagine."
Frank unconvincingly and feebly reasoned his way up a curb, across a pavement, and *Velma'd* his way up a paved driveway which seemed familiar enough. After some flailing, his fingertips discovered the chipped paint of a front door.

Frank patted down his pockets but heard no metallic rattle of keys.

"Forgot the bloody things again."

Luckily this wasn't the first time his ageing memory had failed him, and because of this Frank had learned how to pick his own door, it was simple enough once you *got to know her quirks*. His hand ran down the face of the door to find the metal handle and upon its success, his palm pressed against the brass doorknob only to find the radiation from the sunbeams had made it unbelievably hot.

"Fuck!"

His hand yanked away from the glowing metal, but a layer of skin from his palm remained on the roasting surface, *Iberico ham*. Reactively, his other hand formed a fist and rushed itself into the middle of the door, letting out a woody thud. To Frank's surprise - and relief - the impact of his meaty fist swung the door open, and Frank hurried into the hallway, he was so glad to be out of the blinding sun that he eagerly shut the door behind him to block any of the sweltering heat from entering. He pressed his back against the door, it let out a 'click-thud'. Frank let out a relieved sigh and began to remove his slippers. He was already anticipating his wife calling down to him to 'take off your shoes, unless you want to buy us another carpet'.

"Perhaps I do," Frank mumbled "Perhaps I'll buy a brown carpet this time, that way any mud tracks would be concealed, no more worrying about keeping the carpet a perfect 'just-so' off-white colour."

He laughed to himself knowing full well who made the carpet-purchasing decisions in the house. He jested, but Frank maintained an appreciation for his wife's request, he was grateful to have every part of her. Of course, why else would he have married her? Neither of them was born into a *flush family* so there was no financial advantage on either side, just a security guard and a warehouse assistant teaming up against the world. His eyes dropped to his muddy slippers which contrasted against the pristine carpet and a corner of his mouth lifted. Franks little daydream was shortly broken however when he heard a voice come from upstairs.

"Hello?... Is... Is somebody there?"

It was a timid voice, a nervous voice, an <u>unfamiliar</u> voice. It was indeed a woman calling from upstairs, but it was not Frank's wife. His eyes widened and his heart pounded hard against his chest, *must cut down on the red meat*. Looking around the hallway he could see unfamiliar coats on the rack, alien shoes by the door, and curious paintings hung on the wall, certainly not the paintings he and Sarah picked out. The realisation crashed over him and his stomach felt empty, it all came back to him, and he knew this was not his home.

I need to leave before I frighten that woman near to death, the poor thing must be sitting upright in her bed, improvised weapon in hand, imagining all sorts of golems and villains waiting for her at the bottom of her stairs. Or, perhaps, I should call out to her and identify myself as no threat? I could explain that it is a simple misunderstanding, maybe she would offer some tea in exchange for some security advice. But no, stupid fool, things don't work that way anymore, only malevolence would remain here any longer than needed. Best go, before she sees me and thinks I'm some sort of ne'er-do-well.

Frank slowly, and as quietly as possible, removed his coat from the hook, fumbled it between his hands for a moment, then headed out, closing the door behind him with the faintest of clicks.

He scurried back down the driveway, paying attention to the ground to avoid anything that may produce more sound than necessary. Frank didn't look up until he got out of earshot from the house. A great sorrow filled his heart, which proceeded to pump the melancholy around his whole body, making him feel very heavy, as if he were made of crumbling rock. He inspected the burn on his hand, which was already forming a large blister. It was a yellowish white at the centre which turned to an anaemic pink at the margins. He pressed it to feel the severity of the swelling, it was as if he were holding a flat stone against his will. The pain of the burn forced him to realise that the sun was no longer razing everything it touched, and his neck creaked his head to look towards the sky. However, his line of sight didn't get as far as the sky, as Frank was immediately distracted by his surroundings. Although Frank had barely scurried a couple of hundred yards from the house, he was in a completely unfamiliar place.

"What is this? I ran straight from the house back to what should be the turning of Connaught Lane, I'm sure of it, positive. No road, no amber streetlights, no rows of trees. I've taken all the same steps, why am I not where I should be? Why am I amongst this bricolage of plazas, towers, fountains, and framework?"

His brow furrowed and his shoulder dropped, he recreated his steps in his head, trying to find the point which caused him to get lost, but he was adamant that there had been no missteps. As he was trying to calculate the preposterousness of his situation, he heard a splash come from behind him. Frank span around *quick as a flash* and his hands tensed by his sides, one more swollen than the other. He saw that behind him, too, was a collage of fountains, plazas, and towers - all of which folded into one another while simultaneously pulling away. These *concrete knots* both wrestled and embraced each other as the monoliths battled for space in the area. Towers curled over onto one another like stags clashing for the favour of a doe, the plazas contained stairs which twisted to such an extent that they would be unusable to any human attempting to traverse the landscape, it was *enough to make Escher blush*. The fountains spat water in all directions as if it were venom to keep everything out of its space, rebar and scaffolding spread out over the tops of everything, canopying the whole area - including the unlucky clouds, caging the twisted mess forever. Frank felt completely defenceless from all sides. After all, how does one begin to fight a concrete adversary?

He noticed a pigeon bathing in the largest fountain ahead of him and deduced that it must have created the splashing noise. He watched the pigeon bathe and noticed it had an awkward, frantic movement to it.

"It's not bathing... its, thrashing! The poor thing's wing is broken! It's trying not to drown!"

Frank could hear gurgling coming from the now-waterfowl and made a start toward the poor creature so he could pull it out of the fountain. He began climbing on all fours up the *ridiculous* stairs, jumping over the parts which were too derelict to step on for fear of crumbling along with them. Frank was trying as hard as he could to reach the pigeon quickly, but for all his effort his progress was minimal. He heard and then observed more birds flock to the fountain and around the drowning pigeon. Upon landing in the water, the flock arranged itself in a semi-circle in height order, tallest in the centre, behind the sinking pigeon. The choir began and a cacophony of birdsong came from the formation. The droning squawks were a fanfare to introduce Them, announced by the heavy and steady beating of their own wings, three white pelicans descended into the semi-circle. They did not land to observe the pigeon as the other birds had, instead they stared straight into Frank's eyes, emitting an intensity which made him feel incredibly nauseous. His stomach gurgled and he fought the unnatural urge to throw up. He looked away briefly, just enough to let his stomach settle *right side up* and then looked back at the pelicans. He wanted to know what this grand ceremony was all in aid of but before he could ruminate on it sufficiently hundreds and hundreds more birds - all of which were smaller species, but of all different colours and migrations - filled the sky and funnelled down to the fountain like a feathered twister. They perched around its marble rim, they gathered across the concrete plazas, they landed on the tops of the towers and on the iron rebar overhead until there was absolutely no space left, a sea of feathers, beaks, and beady black eyes had arranged itself around the pigeon, which was now decidedly losing its fight against the water. Every now and then, between the thrashings, the pigeon's light grey head would go under for a short while before it breached the surface once more, gasping in a frenzy. It began to gain a morbid rhythm, slowing the tempo with every dunk. All the other small birds that coated the area noticed this rhythm and began bobbing along with the desperation of their dying peer, murmurs started among the flock which slowly became louder. Frank - now stranded on the one piece of stair which hadn't yet fallen away – was shoulder to shoulder with bobbing birds. He felt incredibly disturbed as he noticed the noise the birds were making was a mimicry of childish laughter, *sounds like the playground in St. Margaret's.* They chattered and giggled in naive excitement as they all gathered to witness the last moments of the broken pigeon. The laughter became more animated and childlike, and even some chanting began to ripple around the crowd. Frank covered his ears with his palms, his right ear could feel his blister pressing against its tragus and he shook his head frantically, the chanting was relentless, and he felt such pity for the pigeon that he let out a scream.

"Stop it!"

It echoed around the plaza. The anguish which was embedded in its resonance was obvious, his scream came through over all the childish giggling and mocking and startled all the birds so much that thousands of tiny wings began to flap away. The sea of feathers parted upwards and eventually dispersed, leaving behind only silence. His eyes followed the trajectory of the flock and Frank looked up to see the sky being revealed as the birds vanished into the distance. It was covered in a thick blanket of cloud, it was neither light nor dark, but Frank knew deep down it was night again. He knew it was night as he did every other night, he could feel **It** pressing on him again. Amongst the heavy cloud was a spherical indentation moving around above him. He knew that should the clouds allow that sphere which rolled around on top of it to tear its covering, the moon would slowly float down towards Frank and press upon his back as it tends to do in his most agitated moments. He imagined one day the pressure of the celestial weight may kill him. He looked away from the sky to avoid the crushing feeling of the moon on his spine and diverted his attention to the fountain once again. It was still far from

15

him, as was the broken pigeon, but he could see that the three pelicans had not yet left. The three white buoys gently danced in the water as they continued to stare right through him, his stomach turned over once more like an old car engine in winter. From this distance Frank could tell that the pelicans each had unique eye colours, not just black spheres as one would expect from most birds. He could also make out a now-still shape floating just in front of the three birds, mangled, grey, wretched, and drowned.

2

The crusted drool which had soiled both the pillowcase and Frank's cheek in equal measures was acting as the antithesis of the pool of cold sweat which his back was situated in as he awoke.

Frank turned to his side to air out his back, he could feel goose bumps forming up his spine from the draughty room and he lifted his head to wipe the 'sweat' from around his eyes onto his pasty bare shoulder. He laid there for a few minutes in an arrested restlessness, watching the digital face of his alarm clock *like a hawk*. When the fifty-ninth minute reset itself to double zeros the alarm sounded, five AM had arrived once again. Frank hastily shut the alarm off to not make any unwarranted noise at this *godforsaken hour*. In his sapped frenzy he knocked a book from his side table to the floor, it let out a muffled thud as it dispersed the dust from the floorboards. He glanced at the leather-bound tome, it was the bible he had bought a little while ago, he had only looked in it once and never again, *might as well just check the horoscopes*. He was quite happy to leave it to eventually become enveloped in the dust it had just unsettled on the floor, and he continued to lay down, occasionally turning from side to side hoping to shake the day's responsibilities from his head.

Suppose I don't go in today.

He fantasised as he blinked frantically to remove the last of the 'sweat' from his eyes.

It's the same thing day in, day out. Nothing ever happens in that place. I turn up, I wander to and fro, I wait for some reason to rise to an occasion, some crime... some emergency, something to make some use out of me but it's always nothing. There's just nothing. I could have never imagined such a pointless loiter, only broken up by trips for coffee and drawn-out shits in that tiny plastic cubicle. The mind races too much to be surrounded by full cosmic silence. Suppose I don't go in today... ah but what else would I do? Potter around the house the same way, waiting for something to happen here? Pah! And if I don't go in today, rest assured it would be the one day all the delinquents and damsels come out of the woodwork. No, might as well get up... better to have a chance at being useful than to wallow in aimlessness.

His left foot was the first appendage brave enough to exit the warmth of the duvet, followed by his right. When both feet hit the cold wooden floor, it swung the rest of Frank upwards like a counterweight. He wiggled his toes and rubbed his feet together to stop the dust from the floor sticking and stretched his arms up towards the ceiling. He felt his right shoulder crack like usual and then proceeded to the bathroom whilst pushing the small of his back forwards with his hand. He grabbed his glasses from the wash basin counter and cursed them as he put them on. When he was a younger man, he recalled seeing the world so clearly, so vibrantly, with no need for glasses at all. Now, without them everything was out of focus, blurred. Sometimes, he would refuse to wear them, He'd joke to himself about how *sometimes it's nice to see the world as a far-away oil painting*, whenever he did this, he could feel his eyes constantly straining to see the world not as an oil painting, but as how it should be, or rather how he thought it should be. *A professional photograph*. Even with the glasses on his eyes were pained, through the varifocals things were almost too focussed, sharp enough to cut his pupils on, and by the end of any day they did feel as though they were bleeding. Frank constantly worried about going blind, partly due to the eye pain, but more so because colours hadn't seemed as vibrant for about a year now. Everything seemed washed out, too bright or too dull, too grey, or too scintillating. Perhaps he was indeed going blind? Only time would tell. However, blindness would not explain his other senses decreasing too. Food had very little taste to him now, everything smelled stale. He couldn't remember the last time he enjoyed music, at this point it was just *an excuse to market sex to the prepubescent*. Frank finished brushing his teeth with the *flour-flavoured* spearmint toothpaste, splashed some lukewarm water on his face to wake himself fully, and made his way downstairs to feed Artemis, and himself. On his way down, he heard Sarah's voice come from the bedroom, it groaned a low and listless "Have a good day, honey." Followed by the creaking of the bedroom door slowly closing.

"Thanks, I will sweetheart... Yes, yes, good morning, Artemis. Stop barking, be a good girl. Calm down! Shhhh girl, at least let me pass down the stairs so I can feed you. Please be quiet Artemis, Sarah is trying to rest!"

Artemis was as excited as she was every morning to see Frank - and to be fed. She was an older dog but still owned the soul of a puppy, and even after losing her right eye and her right foreleg she was as animated and inelegant as ever. Despite all of Frank's pleading for her to stop barking and calm down, she could not see a good reason to, as both of them were awake now, and she knew that once Frank left for work, she would be alone until the evening.

Artemis finished her bowl of dry food and washed it down with big messy laps of water, then - as she did most mornings - hopped up onto the kitchen table, simultaneously almost knocking the table over and herself back to the linoleum flooring.

"Artemis!"

Frank grumbled, feigned authority, and then let her sit on the table as usual. She stared at his hot breakfast while gleefully wagging her tail. She had learned by now that Frank's appetite wasn't as large as it used to be since the accident. Yet he still cooked the same portions he always had. Two fried eggs, four rashers of bacon, three sausages, and two pieces of buttered toast. As usual Frank got up from the table with only half of it in his stomach, he didn't bother to clear the plate away as he knew Artemis would *clean up* for him, and since he had got into this new habit, he had not heard Sarah complain about it once. He was highly aware that Sarah had been much more relaxed about his general tidiness lately. Beforehand, she would constantly be telling Frank what he needed to do, so much so that anyone on the outside of their relationship who were unaware of their dynamic would possibly have observed Sarah to be bossy, perhaps even controlling. If a passer-by - or *professional earwiggers* as many of the neighbours were - overheard Sarah giving her orders to Frank, they might find it quite humorous to witness a petite, unassuming woman to be getting 'yes dear'd' by such an imposing silhouette like Frank's. The passer-by might even let out a giggle and remark something along the lines of "It's clear who wears the trousers in that house!" and if God was feeling particularly merciful on that day, Sarah's acute hearing would somehow not pick it up. Yes, the outside world may find it amusing that a tall, broad, rugged looking man such as Frank was being bossed around by the delicate Sarah, but this is exactly why Frank married his wife and loved her very much precisely for this. Frank had always been blessed with a domineering impression, so much so that when he joined school as a child, the bullies learned very quickly, and with a few bruises, that he would not be a successful target for them. Whilst he did not have the nature to abuse the gift of his physicality in the world, he did allow it to make him somewhat lazy. The same *loafishness* one might expect from a male lion as it observed the rest of the pride picking up around it. Sunning itself and letting its voluminous mane flow in the breeze while the lionesses hunted and placed their offerings at its feet. Growing up, Frank's mother also played the part of dutiful lioness to his father, who preferred the smell of tobacco on his fingers over dirt under his nails. Young Frankie met many pretty girls who would have happily morphed into his mother over time, but the relationships always ended, usually due to Frank developing a certain lethargy to the idea of a life of ease and tobacco-smelling-fingers. Eventually Frank met a woman who would not simply laugh at all his jokes, reiterate how special she thinks he is, and wait on him hand and foot. He met a woman who had struggled with her life, had faced adversity, and had clawed out of it. She saw Frank as he was, not as an object of unending admiration, but as a man with flaws, and an equal amount of potential. Sarah made Frank work from the very first moment she refused his drink offer from the other side of the bar. For once in his lifetime, he had to get up and approach his object of affection for that night. He was arrogant, with no real reason to back it up, but she could see a sweet, kind man underneath the fragile persona. Sarah made sure that their relationship was not rushed. She made sure that Frank understood that were they to be together, both of them would be picking up responsibilities. There would be labour shared evenly, and the romance would remain in the atmosphere exactly between them. Frank - while not used to this type of commitment - quickly had the epiphany that being somebody's significant other was more of an occupation than an accolade. He was thrilled by the idea of this 'project' the pair would be participating in. Soon enough he had his mane cut into something more presentable and found a way to bring in his share of income. Frank accepted the first job offered to him, as at this point his attitude towards perseverance had only changed according to the part of his world which revolved around Sarah. Junior Security Guard Frank Mossan. Thanks to his job Frank was now a protector and a provider. And thanks to Sarah, he was no longer a directionless Narcissus feeling the breeze flow through his mane, fooling himself with his own dérive, and waiting for the world to be provided before him.

"Be back later, I love you."

Frank called up as he triple-checked all his keys were still present in his coat and his 'Chief of Security' badge was affixed to his lapel before setting off in the car.

It was still pitch black when Frank left for work. He drove at an exaggeratedly cautious speed as he navigated the tarmac bends as they appeared in his fog lights; the illuminated fog added a pale sodium lustre to the bonnet of his car which was slick with dew. It would take a regular driver about twenty minutes to reach the shopping centre which Frank worked at, but these days Frank liked to give himself a good hour to get there as he now drove at such a *snail's pace*. He cruised through town in no rush, allowing himself to see all the buildings and places completely empty, as though he was the only person in the world at that time.

"The Turncoats Pub always looks so strange at this time in the morning, too late for drinking, too early for pool." Sarah and Frank used to spend their early afternoons walking Artemis to 'The Turncoats' and playing a few games of pool. The landlady liked to see Artemis, *soppy little thing*, and Artemis liked to see absolutely anybody. Frank would usually blame the dog for distracting him on his shots, either that or he would state that he was letting Sarah win. He laughed to himself as he recalled how Sarah used to gloat at him after winning, the way her face would screw up, her nose would wrinkle, the odd angle that she would stick her tongue out at him.

"Maybe I should pop in there on the weekend, see how everyone is doing... Damn my eyes! must be the cold weather causing them to sting. Must stay focussed on the road."

Frank looked through his window towards the sky and focussed his widened eyes on the full moon in front of him, a shining silver coin in the navy nothingness with its own sovereignty emblazoned across its face. Widening his eyes wasn't waning the tears, so Frank resorted to rapidly blinking them at the moon. With every close of his eyes, the outline of the cold sphere remained projected on the backs of his eyelids and formed a silver ring. He grew visibly frustrated and began darting his head around the car's drab interior, pointing his ears to pinpoint an issue that he hadn't decided on yet. The wheels made their usual rubbery crunch along the asphalt, the air con made the usual annoying 'ticking' sound which the used car salesman had assured Frank was *completely normal*. He lowered his head until his chin was almost resting on the steering wheel, with just enough of a gap that Frank could still navigate the tight upcoming bend. The engine made its usual hum and clatter, there was nothing out of the ordinary happening inside the vehicle.

"What **is** that noise? Something isn't right, I just can't put my finger on it! A grinding noise?... No, it's more of a whirring... Maybe a buzzing?... Ah damn it!"

Frank pulled over to the edge of the tight bend with the intention of checking the engine. However, before even opening the door, he realised where he had stopped. This was **The Corner**. He didn't recognize it at first because at last someone had replaced the metal crash barrier with a shiny new one. No weathering, no contortions or dents or scratches. It was brand new to be sure. But a memento of the old barrier remained, there was still a faint trail of burnt-on rubber on the roads surface leading into the new barrier. Placed at the point where the tire marks of Frank's old car and the new barrier met was a brand-new flower arrangement with a scribbled-on card affixed.

"Daffodils. Sarah's favourite."

Frank began blinking wildly once again, and once again he could see the silver ring on the backs of his eyelids even through the torrent of tears. Some of the salty droplets entered the corners of his mouth as he began to *talk myself down.*

The eclipse... We went to see the eclipse... I was trying to concentrate on the road, but Sarah couldn't shut her damn dog up. God, the howling, it pierced through my head, shook it something fierce... I only looked backward for a moment to tell Artemis to shut up but as soon as I did, she came flying past me, flailing her four legs in the air as she smashed into the windscreen... Jesus Christ... Once we were at the bottom of the gully, Sarah's eyes, her eyes just stared into mine. She wasn't blinking, she wasn't breathing, she wasn't telling me how much of a 'bloody fool' I had been. Irresponsible, bloody fool. And now what's left for this fool? A suffocating job in a breathless shopping centre, the only point of which is to earn some money so I can feed the last remaining, one-eyed, three-legged part of Sarah. But what else in life does such an idiot deserve? Nothing, I'd only destroy it anyway. The dog's dependence on me is the only thing keeping me from packing it all in, upping stumps and retiring to the pavilion. And that's justice for you, no easy way out for me, no sweet release, vet bills and mortgage to deservedly pay... Damn my stupid eyes! I can't very well continue to drive through a screen of tears. Shake it off, Frank. Work to do.

He sat in his car for another twenty minutes or so, hands on the steering wheel, head towards his lap. He knew he left for work early for a reason.

As Franks 'grinding', 'whirring', 'buzzing' car calmly and quietly made its way through the empty parking lot of the shopping centre, Frank began to yawn and smack his lips.

"I hope Kiri is here already, I can't see her motorbike anywhere."

He parked in the closest spot to the staff entrance and made his way inside. The chipped concrete walls, flickering fluorescent lighting, and over-zealous safety signs peppering the hallway made for a decent respite from the moon *pushing into his back*. Perhaps the walls felt like they were closing in on him, but it was a damn sight more bearable than that waxing ivory sphere invading the back of Frank's skull. He took his coat off and dusted it down before hanging it on the row of empty hooks inside the video surveillance room.

"Let's get these blasted screens on then, eh?" Frank turned on the power to the CCTV monitors and instinctively gave them a good slap with his palm. He immediately remembered the blister his hand sported in his dream this morning and felt a chill down his spine.

"Bloody nonsense, projections of a mad old fool! Ah, cameras one to seven are up and running. Of course, number eight, the most important camera, is giving me grief! Another whack should do it, never found a problem I couldn't fix with a good whack!... Ok, there we are, now let's see... Oh! Kiri *is* here already! She's setting up the coffee stand right now... well where did she park her crotch-rocket? I didn't bloody see it anywhere! It's about time for a boost anyway."

Frank made his way upstairs to the ground floor and walked past the rows of unopened shops, the faux-marble flooring let out a tacky 'clack' as his leather soles drummed along it. As he made his way to the centre of the mall, the arcades converged into a large foyer. His right shoulder brushed up against every decorative pillar on his way. Frank always liked to walk along the walls of hallways and large rooms, even with nobody around, he couldn't help but feel like a

26

spectacle when walking down the middle of any lane. He was not a man who craved the attention of others by simply taking it. He was however, driven by that same attention, but only under the condition that someone could notice him for an achievement or struggle by their own recognition. He often thought of himself as somebody who deserved attention, but never had the social skills to extract it from crowds of people. When somebody did recognise him for his merits, he made sure to come back to that person to bask in their praise over and over. Kiri was one such ego stroker.

All four shopping arcades intersected to create the centre of the mall. When it was first built in the fifties, it was the largest of its kind, and people from all over would come to see the events that took place on the circular stage that was situated in the middle of this grand opening. Winter times would feature grottos, blue firs, candy canes, and green and red costumes. The summers mostly held plays, concerts, and such. The stage used to be one of a kind, which made it very easy to book entertainment. Dancers especially enjoyed performing in the Westroot Mall as the circular shape of the stage allowed them to choreograph exceptional dances which engaged the audience that surrounded them from all angles. The four golden narrow pillars which spiralled upwards met about sixty foot in the air, the giant flamberges joined to create a shape not unlike a birdcage. This was especially favourable for dance companies who specialised in having their performers suspended by things such as flowing white chiffon - or something more aesthetically industrious depending on the nature of the dance. The cage structure was a real thing of beauty in its day and accenting it with marvellous rays of light was the most expensive part of the building. Exactly above the stage, roughly one hundred feet above in fact, was the famous 'Kaleidoscope of Time', a colossal, inverted sun dial made from stained glass of every colour. It earned its name by the fractal patterns the panes of glass were set in, the warmer colours of the glass were spiralling outward from the centre of the dial, while the cooler colours spiralled inwards. You'd often see people take pictures under it because of the way it methodically distributed the light across the ground and up the pillars of the shopping arcades stretching out away from it. Frank was never keen on the 'Kaleidoscope of Time', he always thought it was an accident waiting to happen, the way the dial's upside-down blade pointed towards the ground in a most *damoclesian* fashion. But, if he wanted his usual morning caffeine boost and ego stroke from Kiri he would have to once again step underneath it. Kiri was now the only dancer who took to the circular stage, and 'Kiri's Coffee Cart' was now the only scenery. Instead of red and green outfits, or dangling white chiffon it had percolators, bean grinders, and milk frothers - and it was there in every season.

"I'm here to look into a missing motorcycle, miss, you wouldn't know anything about that would you?"

"Frank! You startled me!"

The two of them shared a polite laugh, Frank laughing noticeably more than Kiri, and they exchanged good mornings.

"So where is it then?"

"Where's what, Frank?"

"Your motorbike of course, what else? I didn't see it in the parking lot when I arrived."

"Oh, yes of course! Don't mind me, I haven't quite woken up yet. Rather ironic wouldn't you agree? I think I'll make us *both* a coffee this morning! You don't mind taking it black, do you? The milk ran out last night and no-where's open yet for me to restock... Yes, I can put an extra sugar in no worries, I know you need sweetening up, you old grouch! Brace yourself, the beans need grinding too, NOTHING QUITE LIKE THAT NOISE TO WAKE YOU UP, EH! You know, I had the strangest dream last night Frank... Well, I can't really recall it now, I know when I woke it was the most vivid thing, but it blurred very quickly. I was exhausted when I woke up, and it felt like I had been sleeping with my muscles tensed up all through the night, the middle of my back still aches from it. I hope you don't mind a paper cup, haven't set up the crockery yet. Anyway, I felt just awful when I woke up, it was like I was made out of concrete or something. Yes, yes... well maybe it's normal for you Frank but you've got a few years on me! Alright keep your hat on, I'm getting to that. Well, I felt so awful when I woke up, and I woke up so unusually early I thought it might benefit me to stretch my body out and walk to work... Here you go Frankie, you're welcome. Yes, in the dark... It's easy enough to navigate, I'm no child Frankie! ...I know you're just being sweet; I'm only teasing you."

Frank let out a warm smile, lifted the paper cup to his nose, took in the earthy aroma rising within the steam, blew on it a few times, then took a satisfying gulp.

"I'm surprised I didn't spot you on the road when I drove in, you must have got here at some hour!"

"Oh, very early indeed... More sugar? Yes, it might as well have still been yesterday when I got here."

"Well, you're lucky you don't require beauty sleep yet! Anyway, I can see Ms. Jupeau's opening up her shop now. Won't be long before the rest of them start arriving then, better finish my floor walk and unlock the entrances. Thanks for the coffee as always, I'll speak to you later, Kiri."

"Oh! And Frank."

"Kiri?"

"I saw your colleagues come in a minute ago. They're already bickering like couple of children over politics. Honestly, I don't know how they find it so riveting. Such a bore!"

Frank rolled his eyes at the thought of his two junior security officers, one not-so junior as the other. He could picture them now, discussing policies, rights, freedoms and the like.

"God, they do give me headaches, you know, Kiri. I've half a mind to hide down here and serve coffee with you... Yes, you're right, I probably would make a mess! I'd probably drink more than I sold too! Pah, well, although it's a shame I have to hear it all day, I suppose it's nice to see people be so passionate about current affairs."

Kiri was simultaneously putting the rest of her equipment in order and trying to count the float from the till in small change. With her concentration focussed on her hands grouping up various coins and notes, her thoughts were left to escape her mouth with very little editing for social etiquette.

"Current affairs! Hah, that's a laugh. It's just a way for people to feel as if they're fixing something without getting any oil on their hands. Honestly, I mean, people squabble about this all day, they squabble about who's got the people's interests at heart, who's got the knowledge to increase prosperity, who's got the character of a proper leader – whatever *that* means. They argue about it while they're at work with their colleagues, they argue about it at home with their families, and when there's nobody around to argue about it with, they materialise fictitious arguments in their heads, ones in which they always have the perfect rebuttal for because their opponent is a propagandised caricature of what they consider the enemy. They'll think about it all the time once they've put a wedge between themselves and their colleagues and loved ones. It's all an exercise in narcissism, Frank. Gazing into a pool to see themselves as the only answer. And... And! As if this wasn't futile and pointless enough, Frank. They're arguing about people sitting in ivory towers who only argue these subjects at work! The politicians get *paid* to make these same arguments and they practice, rinse, and repeat the same tactics because if the arguments ever ended, they'd be out of a job! Those two in your office are putting themselves through the same amount of stress and excruciating projection for *free!* Hah! All this bickering to keep the whole charade up. They don't care about us, Frank. They say they do because they believe they're good and true, but really, it's a justification for earning a living through arguing. And your poor colleagues are letting themselves get tangled up in it, wrapped up in its web, waiting for the eight legs of progression to tippy-tap its way over to their stuck bodies so the mouth of power can swallow them. Best to stay well away I reckon, Frank. Nothing ever changes with them so what's the point of trying? Best we can do is scrape by so we can afford their taxes. Everyone in this world is out for themselves anyway, eager to take whatever they can get their hands on."

Although Kiri's words were obviously bleak, defeatist, and morose. Frank found himself very attracted to her in that moment. She was counting pennies, locks of her hair were

31

falling out of her bun, dark circles under her eyes. She was so close to giving up completely. He had lately been toying with the idea of just giving up. Walking out to sea and letting the waves crash over him until he was no longer present to feel them crash. As she was talking, Frank noticed the way her apron tied around her waist and accentuated her curvaceous frame, he realised he rarely saw her smile, and he had the brief notion that if he could make her smile, she might not see the world in such a dreary way, she may even see him as someone who could change the way the world looks for her. Perhaps he could do just that while having his hands rest on her hips. As she finished her thoughts, Frank angled his head to catch her eye, smiled, and spoke.

"What about me? I'm not just 'out for myself', I'm not just 'eager to take whatever I can get my hands on'."

Frank tried his best to flash a warm smile her way, but it was broken quickly when Kiri – without looking up from her till - replied.

"Well... You come and get free coffee every morning from me, don't you?"

Kiri continued sliding pennies from the counter into her palm and updated her tally. Frank silently left the coffee shop and began to do his final security checks before unlocking the doors to the mall. He barely raised his vision from the floor and his half-polished shoes at all.

3

Frank's leftover sausage-halves and bacon were the first to go. The minced pork of the greasy torpedoes needed very little *chomping* before it could be tossed back to slide down Artemis's *greedy gullet*. The beans followed, easily slopped up by her *licky tongue*. The sugary tomato sauce of the tinned beans was all over her *fuzzy little snout* and Artemis felt that she had again been a *good girl* once the plate had been lapped 'clean'. She began to dismount the kitchen table and tentatively placed her only foreleg onto the chair seat before clumsily *plopping down* onto it. The process had to be repeated once more from the chair, then she was finally on the black and white tiling. After eating, her master would usually head over to the metal bowl-thing under the windows, just next to the *fridge*. She knew the word *fridge*. Once she had arduously hopped up to the counter from the tall shiny leftover holder, via the stinky boot holder, she didn't understand what all the fuss was about. All that was laying in there were plates that Artemis had cleaned a few days ago, although now they were sitting in murky, bubbly water. She leant down to sniff at the water and the tips of her *lovely floppy earys* dunked into the water. It smelled odd, like the things that stood up along the edge of the *bathtime.* She shuddered as she remembered the *bathtime.* Artemis washed down her breakfast of sausage, bacon, and beans with a few laps of the frothy, tangy water. The taste reminded her of *No! My good perfume! Bad girl!* It definitely tasted like *bad girl.* In fact, the *bad girl* water started making Artemis back up along the kitchen counter as she dry-heaved a good few times before finally the *Oh no! Not on the new carpet!* Flew out of her mouth, the chunky bits of unchewed sausage held together by springy casing and long strings of bacon fat - which tasted far spicier coming out than they did going down - spattered up the clean plates in the metal bowl thingy, it dripped off the counter onto the tiling, and it congealed in the *bad girl* water. She continued backing up, *hopping like a reversing bunny,* so she wouldn't get any of it on her *funny little paw. Daddy's little Reliant Robin* was now wheezing, sputtering, and reversing at full speed along the kitchen counter, all the while leaving a trail of greasy sludge out of her *toothy bonnet.* Artemis panicked as it seemed like her stomach would never finish purging. Artemis's behind was knocking all sorts of appliances and knick-knacks to the floor. The mug tree was the first casualty. As it hit the tiling, ceramic shrapnel scattered across the kitchen. The shards of 'World's #1 Husba-' and '-th wine. sometimes I even put it in the food!' only furthered Artemis's dismay. She turned about on the polished granite surface and her feet slipped out from under her. Before she knew it her *lanky leggys* gave way and splayed out across the worktop, her right hindleg knocked into the metallic popping machine that Frank liked to put his morning bread in. The chrome-and-grey box was knocked onto its side and it quickly slid towards the metal bowl thingy with the *bad girl* water – bread letterboxes first. It splashed right into it and made a much louder 'pop!' than Artemis had heard before. It went 'pop!' again, and again, then the spot where the chrome-and-grey machine's *tail* joined into the wall popped, banged, and sparked. The sparks fizzed up the wall and hit the curtains above the metal bowl thingy, they quickly set ablaze - and although Artemis would usually sit beside Frank whenever he made this same blinding-grey glow happen in the hole in the living room wall – it was spreading fast, trying to *fetch* Artemis. She toppled off the counter, back onto the stinky boot holder – head first. Once she had righted herself, her claws – trying to gain some traction - scratched along the tiling as she bolted for the front door. The blinding-grey glow had already fetched the kitchen table by the time Artemis got to the front door and the whole house was getting *Corr, it's bloody boiling in here!* Standing up on her hind legs, she used her one front paw to swipe at the door handle and fumbled it around a few times. She missed at first due to her lack of balance, then she started to graze, then scrape, then finally hit the metal handle. The door opened a crack, but in her haste to escape she nosed the door closed again. 'Click' closed the door in front of her, 'fwooooosh' raged the blinding-grey glow behind her as it *gobbled* the whole kitchen and had begun dismantling the wooden stair bannister in between violently loud *growls*. Artemis got back onto her hind legs, the blinding-grey glow now beginning to nip at her hocks. More fumbling with the door... Whimpering, she rapidly clubbed the door handle with her paw. Again, she managed to open it. This time Artemis knew to back up to let the door open a bit more, she let out a loud yelp as she backed into the fire which burnt the hairs on her tail terribly. The mostly bald tail began wagging excitedly as she scurried out the door. Artemis knew that to be a *good girl*, she would have to find Frank, he would be able to *Shoo! Naughty girl!* the blinding-grey glow away. Hopefully he could also fix the roof which had half collapsed into the ground floor...

Although it was still morning, the tarmac had already heated under the sun enough to make it extra uncomfortable on Artemis's *paddy paws*. The discomfort was especially felt on her front leg which had to carry the brunt of her weight – of which there was too much, according to the *vet*. She whined and panted as she hurriedly stomped her front paw over hot tarmac and stray pieces of gravel, some of which got lodged between her toes. She could feel her claws being ground down as she inelegantly galloped down Connaught Crescent which eventually fed into Buckshot Road. Tongue out and ears flapping in the wind, she kept up a steady tempo of barks in-between panting to wake the neighbours, hoping one of them would go and fix the damage to her den. "Someone shut that bloody dog up!" one window shouted as she *woofed* past. Finally, Artemis made it to *The Turncoats*. Sometimes she had to *fetch* Frank from here in the evenings at times when her bowl was empty and Frank hadn't returned yet, she'd usually find him slumped in dark corner snoring away, paper in one hand, glass of horrible smelling liquid in the other. Sometimes he was sleeping so well that he'd *gone and spilled me whisky down me blasted trousers!* Lately, Artemis had had to come here and wake Frank up to take him home most evenings. *Your taxi's here, Frank. Good girl, Artemis.* The nice lady behind the bar would often give her a treat from the big glass jar that sat on the counter. Artemis licked her chops thinking about the treat that awaited her as she trotted through the beer garden past the dry, cracked, sun-bleached picnic tables which had parasols advertising various beers. The grass underneath them was a lighter grey and crunchy while the unshaded portions were slick with morning dew. The hanging sign above the door was creaking in the breeze and the metal bracket was bending under the pressure. The door was locked. No amount of fumbling with the handle could open it, and there was no nice lady behind the bar to let Artemis in, Frank's *taxi* had arrived but the passenger was nowhere to be seen. She circled around the perimeter of the pub, sniffing at – and *claiming* – the neglected flower beds surrounding the building like a muddy moat. She got back round to the front door; it was still closed. She turned and began to circle the pub in the opposite direction. The flowerbeds still smelled like hers going back the other way, this was *good girl*. In a trice, her left *lovely floppy eary* raised at the sound of rustling in the oak tree. A few acorns dropped to the ground and Artemis saw one of those bushy tailed things moving across the branches. It zipped down the solid trunk to retrieve it's dropped valuables. Sniffing around on the floor for them, it hopped over dead branches and empty beer bottles as it tried to locate the acorns. Further and further from the tree trunk the bushy tailed thing hopped as Artemis looked on, stiff and alert. Her singed tail wagged uncontrollably as the creature got closer to her, and further from the tree. It stood on its back legs to get a better view for the acorns among the long, unkempt grass. Its nose twitched and made its whiskers echo with a slight waggle. The chunky little rodent turned its head and it locked eyes with Artemis, who in turn let out an excited 'woof!'. Had the bushy tailed thing known it was dealing with a *furry tripod*, it may have retreated back up the oak tree. However, on the assumption that it was indeed within close proximity of a fully quadrupedal predator, the tree seemed too far for a safe retreat. It panicked when Artemis barked again, striking fear into the little thing, its terror waxed as it sprinted down the beer garden, back out to the road and scurried down the white dashes in the centre. Artemis - wondering what kind of game her new friend was trying to teach her – bounded after it, tongue flapping, drool flicking into the breeze. Of course, she was no match for the agile creature's sheer speed, but being a good sport, she followed, staying on the pavement – *Ah, ah, ah, Artemis! Stay next to daddy, we don't walk on the road. Good girl.* The pub was barely in the rear-view mirror of the *Reliant Robin* now as it bunny-hopped after its jittery friend - which she had just lost sight of as it turned a corner. She heard a loud 'screeeeeech!' which caused her to stop running for a moment. The noise was followed by a fading low rumble, and when Artemis felt the coast was clear, she walked jauntily around the corner. Artemis remembered this corner very well. She remembered the old metal barrier which used to stand there before it was replaced, she remembered the tyre marks her master's old car left which were still on the floor, she remembered Sarah screaming, the glass smashing, the flashing lights, the sirens, the pain, the crying, the *vets* looming over her, the fluorescent lights hurting her eye, and then everything going dark. She remembered waking up, more crying, fewer legs, no depth perception, and one less owner. As she remembered these things her energy rapidly waned, her ears dropped, and her mouth closed. She noticed a new set of tire tracks chicaning over the original ones, and her new friend, squished in the road. It smelled a little like food, she gave her new friend a few licks, some out of compassion, some out of hunger. As her snout got close to the road, her *sniffer* picked up a familiar scent. It was Frank! But it didn't come from the bushy tailed flat thing, it came from the tyre marks trailing off from it. He was far away, but not unreachable. Her nose rose into the air, Artemis followed the scent trail along the road hoping to find her master, so she could *fetch* him back to fix the house.

4

"Frank! Finished the floor walk early today, eh?"

"G'morning, Frank!"

The two junior security guards sat at the table nestled in the kitchenette of the security office. The table legs were perfectly centred in the black or white squares of the checkerboard floor. At its boundaries – as an attempt to differentiate between a space of respite and that of work – were no standing partitions but simply a dirty, bobbled carpet which may as well have been potato sacks stretched across the rest of the room. Adjacent to the kitchen area, and pressed right up against the margin of *Hadrian's Lino*, was a standing array of monitors, which Frank had already switched on that morning. The guard sitting closest to the surveillance screens, which illuminated him from behind, creating a neon aura that one would expect from a Bond villain, was Mr. Neeler. He quickly discarded his cigarette as Frank entered, it was unclear to Frank whether this speedy reaction was made out of a genuine, or indeed an ingenuine respect for Frank's position as senior security officer. At first glance it would seem that the intention Mr. Neeler had when he took the pain of extinguishing his embers between his fingers before not-so-subtly placing the stale smelling remains in his left blazer pocket was to avoid looking unprofessional in front of his superior. However, Frank quickly had a second thought about this. If Mr. Neeler did in fact respect him, Frank discerned, there would be no need to hide his bad habits, as any judgement or rebuke from his *respected* superior would be considered just and fair. It seemed that it was much more likely that Mr. Neeler hid his cigarette out of guilt, guilt that he had been working with Frank for many years and had clearly let his work ethic decline drastically over the course of that time.

"Neeler, you stink of smoke."

Frank winked as he said this and took a seat with his colleagues.

"Yes, I know sir... Awful, isn't it? It's because of this young scally across from us, he stinks up my clothes all day long with his smoking, the laundry never stops in my house, it cannot! 'Else I should not arrive at work in a presentable manner."

Mr. Neeler shook his head as he said this and aimed an obviously unjust amount of scorn across the table, near the lockers and filing cabinets, where Mr. Lameduc had his feet up, still-lit cigarette in hand and a plume of youthful arrogance billowing upwards from his nostrils.

"Oh, do give it a rest Neeler! Frank doesn't want to hear your pompous twitterin' this early in the morning, do ya Frank? ... See he's about as interested in it as I am!"

Mr. Lameduc took his feet off the table and dragged his chair closer to Frank, who in turn felt obliged to sit at one of the moulded plastic seats.

"Frank, settle a bet for us, would ya? The landlord's visiting today, in fact he's already arrived. He's up in the mall manager's office talking business. He came in to see us first thing though – well, actually he came in to see *you* but you were chatting with your fancy friend at the coffee cart at the time. Well, anyway, so he comes in here, right? And me and Neeler are setting up and what have you. He asks us where you are-"

"I told him I would find you for him." Mr. Neeler interrupted in order to maintain the false hierarchy he had cultivated over the years against his co-worker.

"Yeah, yeah... Neeler said he'd look for you." Mr. Lameduc scoffed. "But *I* told him that I didn't know where you were."

There was a pause for a moment as both junior security officers looked to Frank for an answer to a question that Frank wasn't aware of.

"Is that the end of the story? What am I supposed to settle out of that?"

Mr. Neeler grunted and moved to the countertop where he could pour another cup of bland company-paid-for filter coffee while Mr. Lameduc sighed and buried his head in his hands for a moment before sitting upright and lighting another cigarette.

"So, who gave the landlord the correct answer? Me, or Neeler?"

Frank, at the very least to be polite, pretended to actually think on this for a while before replying.

"I really don't care, or know if there is a correct answer."

Mr. Neeler gulped his coffee in order to make way for the words spilling out of him.

"But of course, there is a correct answer sir! The Landlord owns this whole shopping mall and by proxy everything within it, at the very least he has some accountability for everything which happens in here and has a right to know about those very happenings. I told him I would look for you because he is the owner of our workplace, he is the reason we can earn a living here. Shouldn't it be best that he sees us as a team which works well together, looks out for each other, and even cares for one another? Would that not solidify for him the fact that we are doing a good job and caring for the premises which he owns? That we are keeping order and being upstanding in our word to him that we will protect this mall?"

"A good job Mr. Neeler?" Frank scoffed, "You were smoking at the table when I came in here."

"That was Lameduc's smoke you could smell!"

"Oh, do give it a *rest*, Neeler! Frank could probably see some smoke still wafting out of your pocket! It's a wonder he hasn't gone up in flames yet, isn't it? A great big ball of magisterial flames telling everyone about how we aren't doing our jobs right as he turned to cinders from his own mendaciousness... Oh, I'm only joking Neeler, lighten up! It's going to be a long day if we can't have a laugh! Anyway, Frank, hear me out. I told the landlord that I didn't know where you were, right? Now why do you think I said this? I *knew* you were at the coffee cart, I could have told him but I didn't, so what do you reckon? ... Apathy? No Frank! I didn't tell that lavish busybody because of two reasons. One, he's not my boss, he doesn't sign my cheques and I have no obligation to him. And two, I respect your privacy as an individual, Frank! I know you're down there barking up the wrong tree who - let's face it - is more of a sapling compared to a hound of your age! No but seriously, I know your morning routine, I know everything you get up to whether its work related or not because of these little beauties."

Mr. Lameduc took himself over to the surveillance screens.

"But there's no need for the landlord to know about the ins and outs of your day. That's why I quickly turned them off when he came in, like this."

Mr. Lameduc impulsively yanked the plug for the screens out of the wall socket. All the screens went black and he looked towards Frank for approval.

"You know, Lameduc. That's bad for the screens, you really shouldn't do that."

Mr. Neeler furtively giggled at Frank's assertion towards Mr. Lameduc, which had caused Mr. Lameduc to go slightly red and begin jostling the plug back into the socket.

"Oh, it's really no problem, Frank, I do it all the time! I know it's not the safest way to turn them off but it gets a quick result! That's what we need more of around here, quick results! Things move too slowly sometimes; you know that better than anyone, I imagine. Anyway, look I'll put the plug back in, like so... and the screens will all come back on... Well sometimes it takes a minute, hang on. Shut up, Neeler, all that laughing will give you more wrinkles."

Mr. Neeler, despite the insults being flung at him from Mr. Lameduc, carefully set his coffee to one side and walked over to help.

"Oh, you foolish boy, what did you do this for? Pride? Well give me the thing then... Do you want help or not? I mean, really. Astonishing, you've managed to blow the fuse to every monitor... We'll have to replace them all. Should be working in about half an hour Frank, I do apologize."

"Yeah... sorry Frank."

Mr. Lameduc's bruised ego terminated the conversation with an uncomfortable silence. That moment, the two-way radio sitting on the desk crackled, 'chzk FRANK, CAN I SEE YOU IN MY OFFICE IMMEDIATELY, PLEASE, OVER chzk'. It was Mr. Vernme, the mall manager. Frank rose from him chair, and headed for the door of the office but briefly turned back to chide his colleagues before exiting.

"He must be done speaking with the landlord now. I'll ask him who signs the cheques on your behalf, shall I gents? Get those bloody screens fixed, pronto."

Frank made his way through the back corridors of the mall toward Mr. Vernme's office. These were the corridors that only staff and professional contractors would usually see. *Wholly unesthetic,* bare concrete walls, pipes dragging themselves around corners and over doorways. A stark difference to the outward projection of decadence which was ingrained in the rest of the mall. The only time the public would be able to see this side of the structure would be an emergency evacuation, a fire, a bombing, a flooding, a shooting, a gas leak, or anything else which would require a quick exit. Only then would they see the crumbling corners of the walls, the uneven footing on the floors and stairways, the mould creeping in behind the scenes.

Frank made his way through the labyrinthine corridors, following the painted yellow line on the floor, trusting that the line and only the line would stop him from getting lost in the passageways. As he began to get closer to the private elevator which led to Mr. Vernme's office, Frank noticed that the line on the floor was fading, and becoming more difficult to perceive, and the corridors had slyly reduced in size to the point that one would rather refer to them as crawl spaces. His head ducked under the pipes and vents which blew out spurts of atonal steam. He turned his torso sideways to avoid his shoulders touching the filthy walls. The crawl spaces continued to taper as Frank went on. Just as he resorted to crawling on his hands and knees, he reached a very small opening. It led out of what Frank could now only assume was an airduct, into a small room. As he stood up and cracked his back, he was faced with a beautiful set of double-doors, they were black iron, inlayed with copper depictions of cherubim in flight, blowing horns and scattering petals. Following the engraved petals down toward the bottom of the door, where ten of them formed a *bloody awful pile*, he punched in the code '1t7h07' and a quiet humming emitted from behind the doors, quickly followed by the copper cherubs parting to reveal the warm glow of the elevator. It was lit by two orange globes set in the ceiling, as Frank stepped in, he felt the light embrace him and he could feel its warmth on the back of his hands. His feet - which were always sore – were soothed by the feel of the comfortable purple shag carpet under his soles. He took a deep breath in and sighed as he lent himself against the pink floral walls, if it weren't such a short trip to the top floor, Frank would have probably dozed off in this moment. His innate alertness returned to him quickly as he ascended into Mr. Vernme's workspace.

"Frank! Christ, come over here quickly!"
Mr. Vernme's voice called over from the other side of the long, narrow office. The office had been converted from a mostly unused corridor which led into the roof of the building. The office used to be quite spacious despite its odd shape, and a long purple carpet lay in the middle of the dark

floorboards. Frank could remember how the walls were decorated with luxurious wallpaper which boasted depictions of farmhouses, cattle, and wildlife. Frank only knew these details from memory, as now when one entered the office it was much narrower, with barely enough space to allow the door to open. The whole room had been mutated into a suffocating tunnel from the sheer number of metal shelves and filing cabinets which held legal documentation, archived files, and books about mismanagement. Frank even had to stoop as he advanced into the room as planks of wood had been placed across the tops of the opposing cabinets to create some overhead storage where more folders, and cobwebs could be accumulated. One could no longer see the wallpaper depicting rural life, and the purple carpet was barely visible due to a sea of balled-up draft emails which Mr. Vernme had printed out and discarded.

"Frank, good to see you, come here quickly. Mind your head on the- oh bad luck Frank. Please, take a seat won't you."

Frank pulled the wooden chair out from the *interrogee* side of the desk to be greeted by an alarmed and agitated ginger cat. It looked filthy and emaciated, its eyes were milky and it appeared as if it had never left this office. The cat - being disturbed from its resting place - hissed and swiped at Frank. Even though Frank was a large man, it took some effort on his part to shoo the cat from the chair so he could sit down. The cat reluctantly removed itself from the chair and arduously dragged itself over to the nearest filing cabinet, where it rubbed its cheek and left side against the edges, purring loudly, so loudly that it almost sounded like a dog growling.

"Oh, don't mind that mangy old thing, Frank. She's all talk, grumpy old thing wouldn't hurt a fly. In fact, it would be a blessing if she was a bit more aggressive as the flies are really taking over in here... and the mice for that matter... Excuse the fur everywhere Frank, she's moulting at the moment, and I think she's in heat too, which would explain the sour smell."

Mr. Vernme was sat behind his desk, surrounded by filing cabinets, stacks of paper, and glossy plastic plants. Behind him was a view of the whole mall through full-length windows made from two-way mirrors, and on his desk, amongst, underneath, and on top of various sheets of paper were calculators everywhere. It was as if he either kept losing them, or kept bringing out a new one to assign to a stack of calculations - all of which were half finished and left blinking on the solar display screens. Some were flickering from dying batteries as they had been left dormant for that long. Somewhere underneath the stacks of papers and office equipment came the faint ringing of a muffled telephone.

"Do you need to answer that, sir?"

"Answer what Frank? Oh that... No don't worry about that, it's been ringing for years now, I forgot how to answer it an age ago, and now the damn thing's been lost under all my work. You'll get used to the noise, soon enough you won't notice it at all. Ahem, anyway, thanks for coming Frank, now listen, the landlord's here."

"I'm aware sir, my men informed me just now."

"Ah good, good. Very good in fact. But what else would I expect from my team of eyes and ears eh! Well, anyway he's here- No, he's not here- I mean, he *was* here. He's left now - but he might come back at any moment."

Frank was not unfamiliar with the sight of Mr. Vernme being in a state of stress and agitation, but this seemed more severe than his usual *flummox*, he felt fear coming from Mr. Vernme. He was sweating from the top of his balding head, which was only being prevented from invading his eyes and ears by his dark black eyebrows and the sparse bushels of black hair around the sides of his head. He was a sickly-looking man, who was always *bananaring* his back to get a closer look at the documents on his desk. His pasty cheeks were gaunt, and his suit - although it was the same grey suit he had when he was a young man – had also become paler, and seemed many sizes too big for him. It was as if he were shrinking, either that or his desk was growing, neither of which would be within his control.

"What's the matter sir? You seem more anxious than usual."

"Oh, I am, Frank. Anxious is an understatement for what I'm feeling right now. Jesus Christ, Mother Mary, Holy Spirit-what-the-fuck am I going to do!"

His voice cracked as he squirmed in his chair, cracking his knuckles and grinding his teeth.

"The Landlord, Mr. Yharzervay, Frank. He came here to talk about the rent increase, the profits we had made this quarter, whether or not it would be possible for us-"

Frank interjected.

"He's not asking for more money after the year we've had, surely sir?"

"No, no. Thank God no, Frank! But he did want to initially. You see, he brought his daughter along with him, little thing, maybe two, or five, or ten? I'm not sure but she was young, a child, I mean. Anyway, he explains to me that she will be undergoing surgery soon. It's very complicated but basically it sounds like she's got everything wrong that could go wrong with her. The poor thing, Mr. Yharzervay did tell me what the doctors call it but I've already forgotten, it all started when she got hit by a firework a few years ago. The thing exploded and burned one side of her face, Mr. Yharzervay rushed her to the hospital but by the time they got there the burns were no longer visible, very peculiar... Anyway, over time she began to develop all sorts of troubles. It started with fevers, headaches, nausea, you know that sort of thing. But now that it's developed, they suspect it's epilepsy from the trauma, and it may well be, but that diagnosis doesn't explain that recently she has been developing burns on her arms and legs with no rhyme or reason, and her hair has started falling out. Little girl wears a black wig... or was it a dark brown?... No, I was right the first time, it *is* a red wig."

"You said black initially, sir."

Frank stared at Mr. Vernme as he continued wrestling with the towers of invoices at his desk, while trying to file more of them away with his bare feet operating the cabinets. "Black, you say? Oh... Yes, yes! Well, luckily, we will be able to stay in the black and out of the red, Frank, I'm glad you asked actually. Mr. Yharzervay wanted to raise the rent to pay for his daughter's hospital bills... Oh, I told you that already didn't I. Nevertheless, it's going to cost him a bloody fortune. Well, I handed him the books to look over, he took them up to his loft space above my office and went over them for a while, about half an hour later he climbed back down the ladder and he mercifully said he could in 'no good conscience' raise our rent. He knew it would destroy the shop owners who rent here and he could not bring himself to add suffering to those people to afford his daughter's hospital bills."

"That's awfully good of him, sir."

"Yes... Yes, quite. And it means the bonuses for management can still go out this year, terribly important to keep them ticking along happily as I'm sure you're aware." Frank silently, and impatiently waited for Mr. Vernme's next sentence.

"Anyway, ahem. He said he would visit some of his other buildings in the local area to see if he can find money for the hospital bills elsewhere. Well, he asked me if I could look after his daughter while he was out, you see. Obviously, I couldn't say no to him so I obliged."

"Well, It's the least we could do for him I'd say, sir"

"Precisely, Frank. And that's why I need you to find his daughter immediately."

Frank was suddenly acutely aware of the lack of noise in the office, a very grown-up kind of stuffy silence. In fact, everything in the office screamed stuffy and dull. There were no toys laying on the dark floor, no paper stacks were knocked over in the wake of play, no small muddy footprints tracked across the expensive rug. Mr. Vernme's previous words took the wind out of Frank as he watched his boss stare back at him over his *money-counter's* glasses, wringing his sweaty hands then periodically drying his palms off on the knees of his tweed trousers. Mr. Vernme had been Frank's boss for his whole career at the mall, and because of his seniority Frank had always respected him diligently, but in that moment, Mr. Vernme shrank behind his over-encumbered desk, and his posture put his head below his shoulders as he looked towards Frank, not-so-subtly pleading for his help. For the first time ever, Frank saw how

51

small Mr. Vernme really was and instinctively took the opportunity to tower over him by placing his calloused hands on the surface his boss's desk and craning his neck towards Mr. Vernme to gain his full attention. He whispered.

"What do you mean 'I need to find his daughter immediately'?"

Frank purposefully only paused long enough for Mr. Vernme to stutter before interrupting him and continuing his line of questioning. *The interrogator had become the interrogee.*

"You haven't actually lost her, have you? You haven't *actually* gone and lost the landlords gravely-ill daughter? I know that, my boss, the man I have worked for, for all these years, put my trust in when things got really tough... I know he couldn't be that careless as to lose the child of our landlord, could he? Oh, but what am I saying, of course you haven't! You're playing a silly joke on me aren't you Mr. Vernme, entertaining the child with some mischief, eh? Now, which cupboard is she hiding in..." Frank sarcastically skipped across the narrow office.

"This one? Or perhaps she's nearest to the door, waiting to jump out when I go to exit, eh? Or is she behind those drapes? You usually have them closed don't you, usually you say the view overlooking the people in the mall distracts you from your work. Pah! You'd have to get up earlier in the morning than that to trick me sir!"

Frank moved behind the desk towards the window, pulled the drapes aside swiftly and, with a hollow hope, braced himself for the force of a small child to jump out and grab him at the ankles. But he was greeted only by some dust bunnies he had disturbed which bounded over to the base of Mr. Vernme's chair behind him. Frank thought the squeaky casters on the chair almost sounded like whimpering. The casters were not the source of the noise, he followed it up, past the chipped copper-coloured base, to the scuffed and slightly-ripped studded leather backrest, from the other side of which Frank heard.

"What are we going to do, Frank?"

As his anger waxed, Frank thought long and hard about his next actions. The back of Mr. Vernme's *soot-balled* head barely peeked above the executive chair it was cowering in. Perhaps enough of his head was exposed from the chair to allow Frank to quietly remove the curtain railing from above the window and bludgeon his negligent superior with it. 'No, no. Too messy.' He thought. Then perhaps he could simply heave the wheeled chair with all the speed its casters would allow and - with Mr. Vernme still *shvitzing* within it - force the whole thing and the wretched clammy man through the window panes. Obnoxious chair, jagged shards, and meek little man all plummeting four or five stories down towards the circular stage. Maybe with some luck Mr. Vernme might even knock his head against some of the golden framework of the birdcage on his way down, he'd probably land on the coffee cart or even Kiri, but in that moment, Frank didn't find that image as awful as he would usually assume he should. A small grin appeared on his face as he imagined the destruction, and the collateral damage, but it was pure fantasy and he knew it. 'Too much of a spectacle.' Frank reasoned. Maybe the best thing to do would be to simply strangle Mr. Vernme from behind, 'It would be quiet'. He pondered on this for a while without moving until suddenly he felt his left foot take a step towards the chair. He made his best effort to place his foot back on the floorboards without making a single sound, and as his rubber-soled heel ever-so-slowly contacted the dark oak he heard a loud and reverberated *click clack* of women's shoes sound out from above him. His eyes widened and he froze in place, his face felt very hot, and his palms instantly became as clammy as his cowering boss's when he heard a lady's voice whisper from the attic.

"You know that won't help you find the girl, Frank. She'll probably disappear as soon as you lay one hand on that man."

Frank blankly whispered.

"Sarah?"

His neck persuaded his reluctant chin upwards and – with eyes still wide, and pupils wider still – he saw that the hatch in the ceiling had been opened. He couldn't see much from the angle he was looking, just a segment of the A-frame and the cobwebs which had gathered, but he did notice the way it was illuminated. The inside of the attic was barely visible, but it would have been totally pitch-black if it weren't for the faint flickering of a candle somewhere in the back of the landlord's occasional office. It flickered constantly, as if the draught up there was ceaseless. Intermittently it would turn completely black, and he would hear the unmistakeable sound of *those silly shoes she loved to wear* tap across the ceiling, followed by the striking of a match and the return of the dim light source.

"Come on Frank, use your head, not those meaty hands of yours. There's a little girl out there, scared, and looking for her father. Honestly, if I weren't here to keep you in check..."

Frank's eyes were blinking uncontrollably, and he clenched his mouth to stop the quivering.

"You know I'd be lost without you my love, why don't you come down here and we'll look for her together?"

"You know I can't do that, silly old fool! There's no ladder that leads out of this office, and even if there were, I'd never make it down the thing in these heels."

Frank's clenched jaw began to tremble, his anger had passed its zenith and had now crashed into a gentle tide of melancholy.

"Frank! Are you paying attention?"

Mr Vernme's nasal voice brought Frank back into the room,

"I said what are we going to do?"

Frank's eyebrows raised up as he processed the audacity of Mr. Vernme's question.

"What are *we* going to do?" Frank replied "No, no, no! Mr. Vernme, I think *you* have done quite enough already. Quite a complication your predictable negligence has got us in wouldn't you say? Yes, you've done enough alright. But I'll tell you what *I'm* going to do, *I* am going to go and find the Landlord's child. Not because you asked me to, you couldn't care less about the little girl, you're only worried about saving your neck and your pockets. And I'm not going to find her because she's the Landlord's daughter, either. He was foolish enough to leave her under your watch, expecting that you would do anything other than that which is in your nature. No, I'm not doing it for either of you. Apathy on both sides of the coin and the little girl was supposed to call heads or tails. I'm going to find her simply because I know there is a lost child out there who needs to be found. Before I gladly leave your office, Mr. Vernme, tell me, what does this girl look like?"

"Well, Frank... She's... Well, she's a child, of course you knew that. Um- and a girl, which we've also previously established. She's between the ages of one to ten years old, or possibly older come to think of it. She wears a wig which

55

may be brown, or black... No, I was right the first time, definitely red. She could have only got so far; she must be in the mall still. Now let's have a think, what do children like? Oh, she's probably set off straight to the hardware store I'd imagine!"

"The hardware store?!" Frank exclaimed "You really have been up here crunching numbers and cooking books for too long, Vernme. What child do you know that would ever want to visit a bloody hardware store!"

Frank shook his head, laughed at Mr. Vernme, and took a handful of jelly beans from the glass dish on the desk.

"I'll start at the sweet shop, it's right by here, the colours, the sugary smell, there's no way any child could resist that."

Frank made a start towards the door as Mr. Vernme shouted after him.

"Good luck Frank! Find her quick! God only knows when the landlord will be back!"

Mr. Vernme let out a big exhale as his shoulders loosened up again, and he returned to his numerous calculators and sea of receipts, happily working his way through them again he thought to himself, 'well I'm glad I successfully delegated that task to the right man. Frank will soon deliver that little boy-err girl to the landlord and that will be the end of it. If he doesn't find her, we're sure to be in financial trouble... suppose I may have to cut Frank's pay to compensate for the damages.'

Frank reached the elevator at the end of the office to begin his descent to the ground floor of the mall. This time, however, he was not greeted by copper cherubs blowing horns and scattering petals. There was no disguised ornate keypad, nor were there double-doors at all. Frank sombrely pulled aside the steel trellis - which squealed a metallic despair upon doing so, *someone get some oil on this fucking thing.* – it seemed the only purpose of the trellis would be to stop somebody from taking a running leap into the elevator shaft and gleefully plummeting to their bitter end. He stepped inside, using his hand to shield his eyes from the single spotlight on the wall which blasted out a blinding cold light. The soles of Frank's shoes reverberated off the brushed aluminium floor and bounced around the brushed aluminium side panels of the lift. He pushed the 'G' button and promptly removed his hand as he received a light shock from the brushed aluminium button's poorly-wired electronics. Rubbing his palms together and repeatedly breathing into them, he shivered, which made it even more difficult to maintain his balance as the elevator jutted, stopped and started its descent, and even outright fell occasionally as the crooked thing rappelled its way to the ground floor of the shopping centre.

5

The elevator was still muddling its way down to the ground floor when Frank forced the doors apart and forced his exit of the *death trap*, he was convinced the *rickety old thing* would continue dropping past the ground floor and plummet him into the centre of the earth should he let it. He found himself in one of the more neglected and dusty offshoots of a lesser-trafficked arcade. Frank's security staff rarely patrolled this area, mainly because the majority of the shops were closed and boarded. But, despite the inconvenient bearings, Frank could see that the offshoot led to the southern arcade which boasted many eateries, delicatessens, bakeries, and - most pertinent to Frank's plan – the sweet shop, Confectionaire. Miss. Jupeau was the owner of Confectionaire, Frank found her to be an unusually tall woman, and equally as unusually skinny - especially considering her place of business. Her skin was so pale it was practically translucent, and she always looked lethargic. Frank always referred to her as 'Dear', which amused him greatly. His reason for this nickname was due both to her poor timekeeping and her physicality, she was always running late and consequently always running. The way her *spindly limbs* bounded around as she rushed to open her shop every morning reminded Frank of a startled doe, hence the name 'Dear'.

On his way through the offshoot into the southern arcade, Frank passed various boarded-up windows and painted-over signs, the air felt damp, and there was a thick layer of dust coating everything in the stuffy corridor with a dark grey duvet. He heard a door slam shut ahead of him, and stopped inspecting the dust and boards - which reminded him of *the back of a mover's van* - long enough to look up. Frank noticed Mr. Neeler exiting a dimly-lit shop, followed by a cloud of dust from the door's *carpet beater impression.*

"Neeler?"

Mr. Neeler's spine went from flagellum to flagpole.

"Frank! W-What are you doing down here?"

"I was just about to ask you the same, Neeler."

The two of them shared a moment of silence, waiting for an answer from the other, before Frank's head tilted, his eyebrows raised, and his eyes *pulled rank* at Mr. Neeler.

"Oh! Well... Asking for donations, Frank."

"Donations? Whatever for? And from whom? There's nothing open down here."

"Well, almost nothing, sir. The Toy Shop's the only thing still carrying out business in this offshoot."

Mr. Neeler pointed to the door he just exited from, it was made from gnarled wood and painted black, as were the window frames which housed frosted glass, while the faint flicker of gas lanterns shimmered from within. By its appearance, Frank thought the whole shop may as well have been covered in coastal fog and have *sea shanties faintly escaping from the windows.*

"It was the closest place I could think of which might have donated some batteries to us, sir."

"Neeler, stop being so bloody vague, what are you doing down here?"

"The blasted monitors in the security office, sir. Mr. Lameduc thinks he's fixed them now - after vandalising them this morning. He's checked the wiring, replaced the fuses – most of them looked burnt out – and now he wants to see if the job is done. Only trouble is the remote control to turn the cursed things back on has run out of batteries, so I'm seeing if I can procure some to test if the monitors are indeed fixed."

Frank realised while listening to Mr. Neeler that his mouth had started hanging open halfway through his colleague's explanation, he shook his head, closed his mouth and stared at Mr. Neeler with false pensiveness for a while.

"Why don't you just buy some batteries rather than going shop to shop asking for hand-outs, Neeler?"

"Buy some?! But, whatever for, Frank? Why should the security department have to dig into their own pockets for batteries? The whole shopping centre, everyone who sets foot on the premises, all benefit from our services, sir. Why should it fall on us to not only ensure the security and safety of the people, but also fork out for the maintenance of our service? People should feel relieved that they can give something in return for their safety, let alone the feeling of wholeness which can be found through such generosity."

"But we have a budget for such things now Mr. Neeler, I know that you've been here almost as long as I have and remember what it was like before the centralised management took over, but we don't have to busy ourselves with such trifling matters anymore."

"Pah! Central management can't be relied upon, Frank! You know that as well as I do! Besides, our contract sits with the Landlord... No Frank, I don't care what Mr. Vernme says, our agreement is with the Landlord."

Frank's eyes rolled to the back of his head and he started to rub the back of his stiff neck.

"Mr. Yharzervay doesn't sign our cheques anymore, Neeler. He hasn't for a long time. You know that."

"That has no weighting on my loyalty, Frank. And it shouldn't have any weighting on yours, and for goodness' sake don't say his name like that - somebody might hear you! You must refer to him as simply 'The Landlord'."

Frank was aware that he must be visibly tired of this argument by the way Mr. Neeler started to reinforce his statements, as if he were a boxer, swinging at a *gassed-out* opponent. Frank waved his hands in front of him and put an end to the conversation by rummaging in his trouser pockets and placing some loose change into Mr. Neeler's palm.

"What's this, sir?"

"A donation, Neeler. Now stop being a nuisance, go and buy some batteries and don't radio me until the bloody monitors are fixed."

Mr. Neeler gave a 'yes sir' before scurrying off towards the nearest stairwell leaving Frank to make his way past the mounds of dust and sets of boarded up windows towards Puerillo's Toys.

As Mr. Neeler's arm extended, his blazer sleeve crept up his wrist and exposed the olive jade stone which was set in his gold cufflinks. The ivory shirt cotton was sandwiched by noble metals as - acting as the bottom slice of gold – a Rolex coiled around his chalky wrist. The metal band pinched and plucked at his greying arm hairs which Mr. Neeler found oddly invigorating, *keeps my mind awake and my eyes open.* He'd often repeat that same mantra whenever someone asked him about the exclamative inhalations he'd frequently let out. When his chipped manicure started to push open the dirty, once-beige fire door which led to the stairwell, he saw through its narrow, mesh-reinforced window a group of young boys huddled in the concrete-grey, *profane* corner. He very slowly, as not to *disturb* the boys – or more truthfully, alert them of his presence – opened the door. Paying attention to the correct speed and force to apply to avoid any squeaks or intrusive scrapes from the ramshackle door. Mr. Neeler slid his way through the smallest opening he could manage. His bulging eyes were the first items through the threshold which were promptly followed by his neck, then spine, then the rest of him. Presumably, had Mr. Neeler owned a tail, even this would have entered the stairwell before any of his limbs. His head lowered and his knees bent down slightly as he skulked towards the backs of the boys, there were three of them, two of which were of average builds and using the type of language that Mr. Neeler would expect from *ne'er do wells who loiter in stairways*. The two with *sailor's tongues* were egging on the third boy - who was a much meeker stature in comparison, and had the anxious body language to match - to graffiti something on the wall. Mr. Neeler couldn't make it out yet as the delinquents' *nylon draped* shoulders and *greasy, intrusive* heads obscured the majority of it.

As soon as they notice me, they'll run, Mr. Neeler thought as he got roughly an arms-length from the scoundrels, *I'll grab the little fat one, he's too nervous to run, and what's more I'll bet the filthy little toe-rag would sooner soil himself than attempt any form of physical exertion.*

Mr. Neeler spring-loaded his old knees and raised his shoulders, his head tilted down as his eyes widened in unison with his grin, which bore his unusually angular teeth. One would rarely witness Mr. Neeler smile, and it was because of these oddly sharp teeth he had. He would much rather people thought of him as a serious and just man than a *dagger-mouthed Mammon.* He often worried that people would conclude certain prejudices from this exterior, especially Mr. Lameduc whom he worked with so closely. He worried so much about this that he would split their work at any opportunity possible. This was his reasoning when he suggested to Mr. Lameduc that he would go in search of some batteries on the ground floor of the mall, while his colleague should patrol the upper-floor – where the higher value shops were positioned - keeping an eye out for shoplifters and such while the monitors were offline. And luckily for Mr Neeler the monitors at this moment - while he was advancing on his *prey* - were offline, hence Mr. Neeler's tooth bearing.

Just as the liberating notion of being *off camera* was swimming around his hunter's mind, Mr. Neeler's snakeskin-clad foot knocked over one of the youths' discarded empty spray can, alerting the boys and causing them to sharply look behind them. One of the more in-shape boys exclaimed.

"It's the cops! Run!"

"Shit!"

The other said mid-gasp as they made a start up the staircase, taking two or three steps at a time in their panicked stride. The third boy – as expected by *the Naga* –

was a deer in headlights. Upon cowering, the seat of his trousers dropped to the floor and – pulling them out of his pockets – the boy used his hands to scuttle his back up against the ineptly defaced wall. It was a series of crudely drawn geometries, cubes, pyramids, and cylinders - all in very basic colours, *mundane continuance* - with drip lines coming off them from the boy's *poor technique*. The shock of the grown man sneaking up on him, coupled with the toxic fumes of the spray paint in this confined space was enough to put the *podgy little tyke* out of breath, he panted and tried to compose himself while incriminatingly rubbing his paint-stained hands against his trouser legs.

"I'm sorry officer, I didn't want to do it, the other two forced me to! They bully me all the time and force me to do these things, if I don't they hurt me, y'see."
He flashed the right side of his face to Mr. Neeler to display the yellow-green bruising which cruelly decorated his cheekbone and eye socket.

"Please don't take me to jail, I beg you!"
The boy crumpled, and began quietly sobbing in a ball on the floor and one of his hands stretched out in front of him in an attempt at protecting his cowering body.
Upon hearing the two *young men* refer to him as 'the cops' and the *talking marshmallow* refer to him as 'officer', Mr. Neeler smirked and straightened his posture to tower over the boy, he quickly removed his blazer to hang over his left shoulder, covering the badge on his breast pocket which read JUNIOR SECURITY GUARD. He cleared his throat in a way that he thought sounded authoritative.

"You know, this is a serious offence young man. Defacing private property can lead to a five-year sentence."

"I'm sorry sir, truly I am, the other boys... I told them I wouldn't do it at first, but they beat me, see the bruises on my face? They hit me with one of the spray cans, that one over there with the dent in it. They beat me around the legs until I knelt, and they stomped me in the back until I did what they wanted. I'm sorry sir, please believe me when I say that I am! Next time this happens – and I knowing my luck there *will* be a next time – I will not do as they ask. I'll let myself be left misshapen, bloody on the floor, I will let them hurt me until I am unconscious, I will let my mother cry over my coffin as it gets put in the ground before I do anything like this again! Please sir, I beg you, do not take me to jail! My mother would be so ashamed of me if you do, she would not be able to look me in the eyes through sets of metal bars. Please sir, please!"

Mr. Neeler looked down his nose to the *untidy heap* of sorrow which begged on the now urine-soaked concrete floor, he clicked his fingers and pointed at the boy's clothes, then to the puddle of *coward's piss*.

"Well then, you had better clean it up before I lose my good nature."

Seeing this gesture, the young lad immediately understood and, still shaking like a leaf, proceeded to remove his knitted jumper and pressed it into the puddle of urine at his feet until it was soddened. The smell of urea blended with the aerosol acrylic which was hanging in the air to create something ammonia-esque. The boy, woollen mop in hand – which was now three times the weight and dripping with *parmesan juice*, stood up to wet the wall, hoping it would break up the spray paint somewhat. As the boy reached up to begin scrubbing the top of a wonky yellow cuboid in his vest, Mr. Neeler noticed a two-way radio hanging from the child's belt.

"What's that?"

Demanded Neeler.

"It's my walkie-talkie sir-"

The unfinished concrete wall's rough surface tugged at the boy's home-made jumper, causing it to fray and unravel as he nervously scrubbed the wall, it was obvious to both parties that the wall was not getting any cleaner but Mr. Neeler wanted to see this pointless exercise through to its conclusion - the complete destruction of the boy's homely knitted jumper, the lamb which was once proud across its chest had practically all been grated off – *might as well destroy the rest of it.*

"-my mother gave it to me, she works in town, she told me if I ever get in trouble, I should get within distance of her office building and call her over the radio. She works long hours sometimes and every now and then I have to go there to remind her it's dinnertime, she works so hard sometimes she forgets to eat and I bring her what food is left from my lunchbox after the older kids have taken what they wanted. I have a hard time at school so my mother got me the walkie-talkie to help keep me safe."

Mr. Neeler stared at the radio and realised it was very similar to the ones the security team use in the mall.

"Is it in range of your mother's office now?"

The boy stopped scrubbing momentarily to turn his head towards the 'officer'.

"No sir."

"Give it to me."

The boy's eyes widened, his nostrils flared, and his lips pursed together, but he said no words.

"Giveittome." Mr. Neeler repeated "Unless you want to go to jail."

The radio tentatively unclipped from his belt, and with glassy eyes he reluctantly offered the walkie-talkie to Mr. Neeler, who gladly took it and turned it over in his hands, the jewellery on his fingers clacked against the black plastic.

"Please... Be careful with it, sir."

"Be quiet... And keep scrubbing, did I ask you to stop?"

Mr. Neeler popped off the back of the radio casing and, just as he suspected, he saw four batteries in fair condition nestled within.

"Aha! Little beauties. The mall provides."

He removed the batteries and placed them in his pocket, next to the money Frank had given him, patted his pocket and sighed at the pleasing jingle the coins made.

"Don't leave until that wall is spotless, you little convict."

Mr. Neeler said as he threw the radio to the boy's feet, some of the more fragile plastic casing shattered off as it hit the concrete. The boy, more frantically than before, continued to destroy his jumper against the wall, which at this point looked more like a clump of white hair pulled from a drain. Tears streamed down his face and he frequently sniffed hard to stop any *goblins* from coming out of *the cave*.

"I'm going to see if I can find your 'friends'."

Mr. Neeler said as he casually walked up the stairwell with his shoulders back, his chest forward, and his chin up. As he got up the first flight of stairs, he heard a faint voice come from below him, which said softly – through sobbing and sniffing - "Thank you, sir".

Mr. Neeler lifted his jacket from his shoulder and put it back on, as there was a spitefully cold draught in the stairwell, his security badge now visible again, he shivered and wondered how the young boy he just left was staying warm in only his vest and trousers. Just as his apathy began to wane, Mr. Neeler reasoned to himself, *Paupers are used to these conditions* he thought, *it's probably better for him like that. Adversity will make him stronger in the long run. I've done him a service, really.*

6

Frank faced the door to Puerillo's Toys, this was difficult to discern by the sign above the entrance which consisted of an unfinished wooden board and crudely painted red lettering. The majority of the nails holding the sign up weren't fully hammered in, leaving crooked iron shoots sprouting from the border of the sign, a couple of which bounced onto Frank's shoulders as he opened the door which, by the looks of it, *must have been designed by Tinker Sawyer.* Frank's head ducked as he passed under the doorway, although he still managed to knock his *bonce.*

"Look, I'm positive I don't have any spare batteries now kindly leave!... Oh! Terribly sorry sir, I've just had one of your colleagues in here asking about-"
Frank extended his arms towards Mr. Puerillo the same way one would if they were advancing on a frightened animal.

"-Yes, I know... Mr. Puerillo, I must apologize for my colleague, his intentions are, well... he has a habit of over-extending his reach so to speak."
Mr. Puerillo was at the other end of the shop, and both men started walking to the cashier's desk set in the middle of the space. As Frank continued, he noticed the interior was in

stark contrast of the shop face. Almost miraculously, it was brightly lit inside, and patches of primary colours were shooting off in all directions on the soft rubbery floor. The walls were decorated by very endearing – albeit rather amateurish – murals of frantic clowns, toothless and smiling dinosaurs, and stick versions of pets and farmyard animals, all of which were painted in *wholly unnatural colours for their species'*. Given the décor, one would be forgiven for assuming that there might be some exciting music playing in the background to heighten the younger customers' attachment to their selected toy. Instead, there was only silence, interspersed occasionally by the air conditioning unit turning on or off which kept a vigilant temperature to ensure that the perfect level of humidity was maintained to preserve the toys' mint condition. Rows of primary red and blue shelving boasted an enormous variety of children's toys, all of which were ordered first by genre, then size, then alphabetically, then chronologically. The price tags underneath each of the toys had an extensive amount of information about the toy's specifications; its history, its compatibility with the other toys in the range, its place of manufacture, its time of manufacture, which materials were used, the designer's name, the original year of release, which edition it was... and so on. However, what the tags – which were each about a foot in length due to the overwhelming amount of information on them, *if doctors wrote receipts* – failed to infer to the potential browser was the price of the product in question. All of the toys on the shelves were sat at perfect right angles, perpendicular to the edge of their respective shelves, and were no more or no less than exactly forty-seven millimetres from said edges. The packaging was predictably in mint condition also, there were zero scuffs or foxing around the edges of the boxes, Mr. Puerillo seemed like the sort of man who would throw such imperfections away immediately. He was a svelte man with blonde hair which, presumably after years of combing and *Brylcreeming* had been disciplined into staying very close to his head, this stylistic choice only made the rest of his angular facial features seem more pronounced. His neck appeared narrow and long as his shirt collar was a couple inches too wide, *a blonde worm after rain*. He floated towards the cashier's desk without making a sound, not even from his dutifully-polished shoes as they impressed upon the soft rubber flooring.

"So, how can I help you, Mr. ...erm-"

Mr. Puerillo looked around Frank's breast pockets for a nametag by which he could properly address the man standing in front of him.

"Just call me Frank, everyone does."

"Very well Frank, well if we are to be friendly enough for such informalities you may refer to me as Alfie."

Alfie smiled an unusually large grin for a man his age. He grabbed Frank by the hand and shook it vigorously.

"Pleased to meet you Frank, I don't get many visitors tucked away down here but it's always pleasant to meet another grown-up. Now, are you here to learn about my toys? I've recently had a shipment of the latest Action Man figures, fully poseable limbs, some of them come with up to three different outfits! I'm sure I could give you one as a gift seeing as we are now such good friends, yes?"

"Actually Mr. Puerillo-excuse me... Alfie. I'm here to ask whether a young girl has come into your shop today? It would've been between nine o'clock and-"

Mr. Puerillo's nose scrunched up and his lips twisted in on themselves as he finally broke eye contact with Frank.

"Yes, she came in here."

"Well hold on Alfie, I haven't even given you a description yet."

"She's the only little girl that's set foot in here today. She clearly doesn't know the rules."

Mr. Puerillo pointed to a small sign which hung above the cashier's desk, ABSOLUTELY NO CHILDREN ALLOWED IN THIS SHOP – EVEN WITH THE ACCOMPANIMENT OF A GROWN-UP.

"See? No children allowed."

Alfie folded his arms and puffed his cheeks out.

"No children allowed? But how do you make any sales? You can't be solely reliant on parents entering - on their own no less - with the intent to buy a surprise gift for their child. How do you manage to sell any stock?"

Frank immediately regretted asking Alfie this question as he saw a spark build behind the man's eyes, and as he started to answer, Frank thought about the question he really should have asked. *The girl, should've got straight to the point.*

"Sell? Sell?! None of this is for sale Frank! Why on earth would I sell any of this?! Why, you might as well ask the Sistine Chapel why it doesn't sell its ceiling. I mean, really Frank, I thought you and I could have been kindred spirits, seeing through the novelty to admire such historic importance and marvel at the achievements in engineering that are embedded within these glorious artefacts."

Frank raised a hand and opened his mouth to speak, but Mr. Puerillo's Hornby locomotive of outrage was in full momentum now, and with his hands held behind his back, only now and again being freed to gesture as that of a conductor, he paced back and forth in front of Frank.

"And now I see that my assumed like-minded confidante has turned out to be nothing more than the rest of the pudding-heads which drag their feet and knuckles in here asking to buy a priceless piece from my collection which I have spent so long curating! Of course, I turn them away, I always turn them away, Frank. For, were I to oblige them and accept their offer of worthless coins and paper, then what would they do with my beloved relics?"

Frank was desperate to interrupt Alfie, but his rolling-stock reproach was at top speed with no sign of slowing down – even if it did some inertia would be expected. As Mr. Puerillo contemplated the answers to his own questions, Frank became speechless at the level of animation and passion coming from a man of Alfie's age and took on the role of ferroequinologist - *train boffin*.

"Oh gods... Frank, you don't think. You don't think they would actually give one of my objet d'arts to their children? But how could I conceive of such a travesty? Small, sticky hands tearing open the boxes to mistreat the plastic-formed Davids within. No, Frank, I can't do it. I won't do it. I will not 'share' these with anyone!"

Mr. Puerillo lent against the cashier's desk, his hands trembling and sweaty. Frank, having lost all sense of conversational tactics after seeing this wild overreaction to something which appeared to be the whole point of owning a toy shop in the first place, put his hand on the distressed man's shoulder and spoke.

"Alfie... What did the girl look like?"

"Oh, I don't know, Frank. She looked like someone who shouldn't be in my gallery! Apart from that I haven't got the faintest clue what she looked like. As soon as she came in here, I got the broom out and swept her back out the door. She headed off towards the centre of the mall. I expect the freeloader would have tried her luck at Confectionaire after."

"Thanks Alfie, I was headed there anyway. Listen, I'm sorry if I upset you."

Frank, fully aware of the time that had been wasted in this 'shop', stuffed his hand in his pockets and cantered towards the door again, muttering to himself the whole way.

Mr. Puerillo stayed by the cashier's desk, and quickly calmed down when he noticed that the buttons on the register made pleasant 'dinging' sounds.

More nails fell onto Frank as he exited through the doorway back into the offshoot, he looked towards the opening to the main atrium and could see the sun dial embedded in the ceiling, it was glowing a pale grey, and it was so eerily bright that it was impossible to read. Judging by the harshness of the natural light invading the mall the weather must have been overcast, and Frank once again felt a pressure on his back. He took a few moments to contemplate the strange interaction he had just had inside the toy shop. What an odd man Mr. Puerillo was, but would it even be fair to call someone such as him a man at all? Yes, his hair was greying at the edges, yes, his face carried the lines of age, and his voice was raspy and world weary, but his actions, the way Alfie darted up and down in a tantrum declaring nobody should be worthy of owning such trivial playthings as if they were his world. Frank rubbed his rough unshaven cheeks as he thought about Mr. Puerillo, *Even referring to him as Mr. seems incorrect, and my pity for him – although justified –*

only increases the endearment I hold for his eccentric manner. But I can't help him now, I've already wasted so much time.'

"Frank?"

His train of thought was broken, and Frank's eyes refocussed into the real world at the sound of Kiri's voice.

"Is that you Frank? Pleasant surprise!"

Her face was blushed as if she had been caught in a compromising situation, had her hands not been busy carrying a plastic tray with a large cup and saucer on it, they may have attempted to cover her cheeks.

"Kiri? What are you doing all the way over here?"

"I could ask you the very same Frank."

She continued past Frank on her path as if what she was doing was so mundane that there was no need for any curiosity or explanation. When she got to Mr. Puerillo's door, she was forced to turn and face Frank – who had not stopped staring – to push the door open with her behind.

"Are you delivering coffee to Alfie? Since when have you provided this service? Although, I'm not sure he should have any to be honest with you, he seems a tad excited already."

"Oh Frank, I've always done deliveries, only to the right people, mind. I know which people need a little extra push, I've been working here forever, it would be a shame if I didn't know that about people by now! And it's not coffee actually, Mr. Puerillo prefers hot cocoa, it helps him with his late morning nap you see. Here, since when has he been 'Alfie' to you anyway?"

Frank fidgeted with his hands and stumbled over his words as he tried to regain some professionality, however, he couldn't help but notice the inquisitive look in Kiri's eye, and the form her body took as she was paused halfway through the door.

"Oh, well... he just told me now as a matter of fact. He told me as if to make a friendship but I imagine he regrets that now that I displayed my ignorance of toys to him."

"Oh, I understand completely" Kiri chuckled, "Well it's probably for the best, eh Frank? People like us can't hold onto friends for too long, and besides, it's not friendship we're looking for, is it?"

Kiri winked at him before disappearing behind the door, leaving Frank a little taken aback, but intrigued all the same. *What did she mean by that?* Frank asked himself as he watched his footsteps push the tiles of the offshoot past him to make way for the marble flooring of the southern arcade. *I can hold on to friends, surely? I mean, sure, I haven't seen any in a while but... Well, we're all busy with work that's for sure. I suppose you could argue that Neeler and Lameduc are my friends - But what am I saying, they're colleagues and nothing more, Jesus, to think I'd even share a pint with either of them before blowing my brains out! What need do I have for friends at my age anyway? Kiri's right, what point is there looking for friendships, it's just another person to let down. Sarah always used to say "A group is as fast as the slowest member." unfortunately, I'm sure she was much quicker than I.*

The left corner of his mouth raised and he chuckled to himself but quickly restored his *poker face* once he caught a hazy reflection of his *goofy and childish* expression in the polished flooring. He shook his head - *jowls flapping like a bloodhound*, and looked up. He could smell a wonderful bouquet of syrups, honeys, dried fruits, chopped nuts, choux pastry, and - his favourite - chocolate. The nostalgic smell wafted out from the wide-open doors of Confectionaire. Frank was glad that this was his destination because he could not guarantee he'd ignore the aroma of the shop, even if it was a detour.

7

"Blasted stairs."

Mr. Neeler was hunched over with his hands leant on his thighs, wheezing. He had conquered the stairwell and was now catching his breath by planting himself at its peak. As the fire door shut behind him, a gust from the stairwell caused the three panels of his blazer to flap victoriously. He took in the view of the upper floor as he half-masted and rested his hands on his hips. After a few sighs, he straightened himself, patted down his shirt and continued his expedition. Still – ambitiously - in pursuit of the other two *little yobbos*, and poorly hiding his panting - he began to scout out the area, muttering to himself.

"Perhaps the department store? ...hmph, I can't imagine what business those ruffians would have to go in there for. Perhaps the record store, they seem the demographic to listen to that canorous nonsense. That's probably what turned them into little vandals in the first place, bloody awful racket it is – when's the last time the cleaners went over this flooring? It's filthy... Oh, they're not open yet. No wonder, the scruffy rock and roller's probably never seen earlier than midday in his life. No signs of forced entry either so my targets haven't purloined anything either – although I wouldn't put it past them."

"Oi! Neeler! Over here!"

"Of course, the jewellery shop! Little magpies must be over that way!"

A few hundred yards away, just outside of the jewellery shop - clearly window-shopping rather than working, stood Mr. Lameduc. He hardly took his eyes away from the trinkets in the window as Mr. Neeler approached him.

"Ah, Mr. Lameduc! I don't suppose somewhere in your busy schedule of sitting on your hands and calculating the minutes left until your next paycheque arrives you've by chance seen a couple of young lads with spray paint canisters, have you?"

"Oh, that's charming, isn't it? Well, it's nice to see you too, Neeler! And with a greeting like that why should I tell you whether or not I have seen anybody matching that description eh?"

Mr. Neeler rolled his eyes half way out of his skull before instructing Mr. Lameduc that it was very inefficient of him to be so sensitive and that he was looking for the aforementioned boys because they had been involved in some fairly serious bullying which Neeler had *swiftly sorted out*. He then wiped his finger across the layer of dust on the jeweller's shop window and inspected it with disdain, rolling it between his fingers as he continued.

"That's why you should tell me, Lameduc, they've been mistreating a younger child. And besides that, we are colleagues and as such should be acting cooperatively."

"We're not colleagues, Neeler."

"But of course we are, you daft man! We work together every day. What else could you possibly describe us as?"

Mr Lameduc crossed his arms and leant his back against the window, briefly forgetting about the layer of dust that would transfer onto his uniform. Once he realised what he had done it was too late to stand up straight as it would have been obvious that he made a mistake, so he continued to lean on the window all while doing his best not to move more than necessary to avoid rubbing the dust further into his attire.

"We don't work together every day. We work alongside each other every day, whilst simultaneously performing the exact same tasks with a different approach. Sometimes one person's approach is better than the other but that's neither here nor there, the point is we don't have to be collaborative at all. Frankly, it's a wonder you're still here, Neeler. I thought when the new centralised management came along, they'd catch wind of the wasted resources and sack one of us. I assumed purely due to your age it'd be you they gave the chop to. Still think that's a possibility honestly. So, while we're both here, and both intending on remaining here, you can't be my colleague... You're competition."

"Goodness me Lameduc, you've really got a bleak outlook on life."

"Perhaps, but I still won't tell you where those workmen went."

"Workmen? I said I was looking for two boys, not workmen."

Mr. Lameduc's eyes darted around slightly before he quickly regained control of them and aimed them downwards to his shoes, he gulped and then pursed his lips to block any more words which may escape. Mr. Neeler glared at him as a disapproving father might do to a petulant child, he noticed the way Mr. Lameduc's eyes darted around even while he clearly wanted them to remain fixed on his shoes. He noticed the way Mr. Lameduc's right hand was rubbing his left wrist, almost as though it were feeling for something. Over Mr. Lameduc's left shoulder Neeler could see an array of glinting watch faces reflecting the windows spotlights out to the walkway, creating a little kaleidoscope on the marble. Mr. Lameduc looked up at his *competition* with puppy-dog eyes and increased the theatricality of his wrist rubbing.

"I'll buy you a watch if you tell me."

Mr. Lameduc's ears pulled his head toward Mr. Neeler instantaneously. Although his immediate excitement was quickly extinguished again.

"The shop's not open yet though. Reckon Mr. Swinnart's running late today. I mean, he's late most days, but today he's *really* late. Must be nice to own your own shop like that eh? If you don't turn up, the only money you're affecting is your own. Still, it's unlike him to be this late."

Mr. Lameduc put his hands against the glass and attempted to look further into the dark, empty shop. Mr. Neeler, disgusted with how easy it is to motivate his *colleague* - and after laughing to himself about the mass of dust on Lameduc's back – unclipped his wristwatch and handed it to Mr. Lameduc.

"Well keep hold of mine until Mr. Swinnart's shop opens, then I'll get you your own. Be careful with it though, it's real gold. I don't want to see it in any other state than this when it's returned to me, understand? Good. Now will you finally tell me about those boys? And why did you refer them as workmen?"

Mr. Lameduc turned the watch over and over in his hands, enjoying the gentle clinking noise the metal band made as it clacked against itself.

"Well... I thought they were workmen at first. Actually, that's not true, I *knew* them to be workmen at first - as that's what they told me they were. I asked them you see. I saw the paint cans in their hands and they were clearly in a hurry so I asked 'Are you workmen?' and they nodded. So really, I wasn't incorrect by referring to them as workmen as those were the facts that were presented to me in the situation. For me to be incorrect about them is just a testament to my trusting nature really... So anyway, they came rushing out of the same stairwell you came from and, after a brief exchange, they told me they were re-painting part of the mall on the lower floor but needed to get some more supplies from the hardware store."

"But the hardware store isn't up here, Lameduc."

"Isn't it? Oh well, there's my trusting nature again! Well as I was trusting that they were indeed going to the hardware store, I asked if they could pick up a few parts for me so that I could attempt to get the security monitor working again. 'With whose money?' they asked... I said with their own money of course."

Mr. Neeler nodded approvingly.

"I explained to them that a couple of hard-working men such as themselves must surely have some cash free for a few extra parts at the hardware store. Well, they insisted that they didn't have any money, and after turning out their pockets I found them to be telling the truth. I did find it very strange that they had absolutely no money, I mean, how is that even possible? There's always some money circulating, there's always a way to get money in my experience. Anyway, after arguing with them back and forth, back and forth about their financial situation I eventually gave them some money to buy the parts with. I told them I'd wait here for them to return and I've been waiting since."

Mr. Neeler shook his head and rubbed his temples.

"They're not coming back, Lameduc. They've gone off with your money."

"Well, I know that *now*, I was just remaining here until the jewellery shop opened so I could pick out a reward for a job well done."

Mr. Neeler, jaw agape – stunned enough to forget his inhibitions regarding his teeth – decided not to discuss the clearly subjective definition of 'a job well done' which Mr. Lameduc held. Instead, he explained to Mr. Lameduc how he had in his possession the batteries needed to test the monitors and that they should make their way back to the security guards office to get the monitors working again. Mr. Lameduc was hesitant to remove himself from the proximity of the jewellery shop but after some brief - and mostly circular negotiations, Mr. Neeler allowed his colleague to keep the watch he loaned him. They started walking towards the staff only area of the mall and Mr. Neeler asked what else they needed for the monitors. To which Mr. Lameduc seemed confused.

"What do you mean?"

"You told me you had sent the boys off to purchase a few more parts for the monitors. What parts were they and why do we need them?"

"Oh! Well, I'm not sure we *do* need any other parts to fix the monitor. I simply asked the workmen to buy me 'a few parts' for fixing monitors. I have no idea what they would have brought back. I just wanted something to show in case central management asked to see where their resources were going. I thought if we could give the impression of competence in a scenario such as an audit, they would be satisfied with how we were carrying out our work."

Mr. Neeler again found no prospect for healthy debate, and instead slowly nodded his head as though pondering on the nonsense he had just heard. As he was doing this, he noticed how incredibly well polished Mr. Lameduc's wingtips were. And, although he knew they weren't part of the official security uniform, he secretly admired them, and wished he had a pair in such a nice condition to call his own - not that he would ever confess that to Mr. Lameduc. The two meandered their way back to the security office and, after a pause in conversation, Mr. Lameduc spoke.

"Has anybody told you your teeth are... very angular?"

Mr. Neeler kept a completely straight face and looked away as he answered.

"Has anybody ever told you to mind your own business?"

Inside the sweet shop the aroma remained just as welcoming as outside, but as Frank made his way into the large space of shoulder-high display units containing sweets and treats which parents were permitting their lucky children to peruse from, seeing the ambitious volume of confectionary the *little darlings* were voraciously filling their cardboard tubs with caused the scent to gradually turn putrid, until it was completely overwhelming. Frank found himself with a tightly shut mouth and he slowly and methodically rationed the air his nostrils were inhaling. Children raced up and down the shop, bumping into Frank's thighs with the intent of racing to the next transparent plastic container holding vibrant colours and varying textures. One slightly older child pushed past Frank with such intent that he was forced to briefly clutch at his hip and wince before he could stand straight again and continue to deny his age. It was busy to say the least and Frank felt like a giant at a carnival, business must have been very good for Miss Jupeau.

"Bonjour mon ami! And bienvenue to Confectionaire! How can I help ze handsome gentlemen?"

Frank blushed a little as it had been some time since anybody had referred to him as 'handsome', Sarah had only complimented him on black tie occasions when he had actually made an effort, *scrubs up well, my Frank*. She was well aware that the cause of his inflated ego when they met had been from women fawning over him far too much in his youth. He appreciated the scarcity with which Sarah gave compliments, as he knew when they came from her that he had earned them and they were genuine. He was caught off-guard by Miss Jupeau, whose peculiar amber coloured eyes were beautiful enough to distract one from the fact that they were perhaps too close together. The way she dominated people's attention with unwavering eye contact had always been a conscious strategy for her. She had learned how to amplify the intensity of her eyes by tying her black hair in a strict bun, and adorning her slender frame with a modest black dress and plenty of jewellery which glared under the shop's spotlights whenever she patrolled her property. Everyone who worked in the shopping mall knew that Miss

Jupeau was not actually French, however her intoxicating demeanour and hospitality encouraged people to play along.

"Hello Miss-" Frank caught himself mid-sentence "Bonjour Madame Jupeau."

He suddenly felt silly and cheap, *une steak and chips sil voo play*. He shook his head trying to release the embarrassing memories of his and Sarah's trip to France. Frank decided to continue in English, and began his following sentence with the type of inauthentic laughter one might use to punctuate a statement which is neither humorous, important, nor insightful.

"Business looks good today!"

"As long as there are children in the world, my business will remain good Monsieur. Is it your first time visiting my joli establishmon? We have everything you could possibly want here, bon bons, macarons, pastilles-" Ms. Jupeau took a brief second to test her knowledge of romantic languages before giving up "-lollipops, gummy worms to gummy snakes, chocolate mice to chocolate elephants! Are you buying for a son? Daughter? Nephew? Neice?"

"Actually Miss- Madame Jupeau, I'm on the clock at the moment. I've come to ask if an unaccompanied girl has been in here this morning."

"Oh, you must mean Ida!"

Frank quickly reached into his blazer and produced a notebook, grabbed a pen from the counter, realised it was a candy cane in disguise, and grabbed a biro that sat next to the register. He quickly scribbled down **Ida** and fired off some follow up questions which Miss Jupeau promptly answered.

"Oh well she must have been about seven or eight I suppose. Very quiet, very shy. Beautiful looking thing, green eyes, red hair, although her clothes were a little plain in my opinion."

She began to fidget with the diamond bracelet on her left wrist and smiled to herself.

"Although I'm sure when she's grown up, she'll have plenty of gentlemen gifting her dresses and jewellery."

"And did you speak to her at all, Madame?"

"Oh yes of course! I was very concerned on the count of her being on her own. She told me that her father will come and get her when he is ready. 'When he is ready?' I said, it is not for a father to be parenting his child as and when it suits his schedule Monsieur!"

"Please Dear, call me Frank."

"As you wish Franc, don't you agree it is not good for a child as young as she to be wandering around aimlessly wiz no guidance? Wiz no sure direction until her father appears out of the blue to collect her? Such apathy for a dependent, I cannot fathom it!"

Frank noticed the theatrical way Miss Jupeau was waving her arms during her monologue and was already tired of the act.

"But Madame, why did you let her leave?"

"Let her leave? Ha! Let her leave?? No, no, no I did no such thing Franc! I tried to make her stay, believe me I did. I asked her about her father and if there was some way for me to contact him but she just looked me up and down and said he would not hear me. Such a strange child, but I suppose that is what happens when the imagination is all they have for company. So, I spoke with her for a while and I could see her looking around my shop with sad eyes, she is so skinny I could hardly stand it! I grabbed some candies and chocolates from my shelves and handed them to her in a bowl to try to keep her for as long as I could. Ida and I spoke for a while longer while she chewed and crunched her way to the bottom of the bowl, but then."

Miss Jupeau looked around her shop with a scowl.

"Her face turned very pale, and she was holding her stomach so tightly, she must have eaten ze sweets too quickly. She began to cry and I rushed her to 'la toilette', the ensuite one in my back office."

"She was nauseous?" Frank asked.

"Judging by ze retching noises coming from the door I should say so, you could hear it out here on ze shop floor!"

"You didn't stay nearby?"

"Well, I couldn't. Mr. Swinnart dropped by wiz another gift for me."

Miss Jupeau turned her head sideways to present Frank with some very shiny earrings. "What a darling he is, always bringing me samples of the new stock he has in. I went back there after to look in the bathroom mirror at my earrings and ze door was wide open, Ida must have run straight past me in my merriment. I turned back towards the shop and both Ida and Mr. Swinnart had vanished."

Frank wanted to enquire with Miss Jupeau about her relationship *wiz* Mr. Swinnart but at that moment Frank, Miss Jupeau, and all the customers and browsers of Confectionaire fell silent to hear the distressed screams of a woman's voice repeating a word. Frank knew the voice was unmistakably Kiri's, and the word was 'thief'.

Frank noticed a change in the interior of Confectionaire when he heard Kiri's cry. What was once enticing sweets, candies, and chocolates, all presented in brightly coloured foils, papers, and tied with vibrant ribbons in bows, were now piles of grey pellets, wrapped up in old newspaper. He saw the children excitedly diving into the packages, shovelling the pellets into their mouths as their parents looked on as if to say 'look at our little angel enjoying his treats, what kind parents we are!' *what kind of parents are you?* The more voraciously the kids scooped handfuls of grey pellets into their mouths the quicker their complexions waned from lively shades of browns and pinks to sickly grey. The sea of little bodies, cross-legged on the floor, with grey skin, in grey clothes, tired eyes, gaunt cheeks, some of which were holding their bellies and folding over. The only interspersion of colour Frank could see amidst the drab chaos was from a few of the children who had been ill and stained their clothes with curiously technicoloured vomit. He looked back at Miss Jupeau as if to accuse her of something, but noticed in her face – and all the other adult patrons in the shop for that matter – there was no reaction to what was happening to the children. The adults were calmly carrying on as they were beforehand, and Frank doubted the chaos he was seeing. Kiri screeched again.

"Thief! Someone stop him!"

Frank made a start towards the door, pushing aside the adult customers of Confectionaire with a little extra *justified* force, and doing his best to not trip over any children laying on the floor, or get any puke on his *clompy* work shoes.

As Frank bolted out of the sweet shop, still shocked from what he just witnessed but reacting to Kiri's cries for help, he glanced back over his shoulder to Confectionaire. It appeared as a typical sweet shop again. Colours, smiles, playful children, happy parents, it was all back.

"You're losing it Frank."

He muttered to himself as he struggled to maintain a steady breath while running towards the column of sunlight which was shining through the Kaleidoscope of Time some few hundred yards ahead, under the beam emitting from the sun dial, and just in front of The Birdcage was Kiri's coffee cart, and a very distressed Kiri waving her arms - *like Olive Oyl.*

"He went off that way Frank!"

Kiri pointed her right *windsock* arm to the west atrium of the mall and Frank followed the direction, his leather shoes rubbing into the tops of his feet every time they slapped onto the marble floor. What was left of his hairline was already damp with sweat, and his knees were trembling from the adrenaline before Frank even saw the culprit. It was a slight man, and Frank could gauge that the thief was likely a foot shorter than him. Through all the sweat, the shaky knees, and the pains in his feet, Frank was wearing a little grin. It had been a while since any *action* had occurred in the Westroot Mall and it was a nice break from the monotony of *business as usual.*

"Poor little fella..." Frank started muttering *breathily* where he could in-between desperate gasps to sustain his pace. "He's got no idea... what's coming for him... Just a small bloke too... I'll show him... How we welcome thieves... In my mall."

The slight man darted behind a corner.

"Bloody idiot!... He's cornered himself now... That arcade's... A dead end... And that elevator's been out of order... for weeks!"

As Frank approached the corner, he began running scenarios in his head. *If the backs turned, headlock. If he's charging at me, sweep the legs. And if he has a weapon?... Pah! They never have a weapon.* Frank eagerly darted around the corner into the arcade, he heard a loud 'Crack!'. Everything went *crooked and wobbly*, and as Frank's legs buckled and he began to fall, he heard manic footsteps getting fainter and fainter. Frank's head hit the marble floor, he felt something hot dripping from his ear, and his eyes closed shut.

8

Initially, Frank felt no need to open his eyes and check his surroundings. He could hear the babble of flowing water accompanied by the subtle hissing of pressurised air escaping. He could smell a freshness in the breeze which only active water could produce. He could feel the cold, crisp water lapping at his sides and splashing up at the centres of his soles. The surface of it rose and lowered again around the contours of his elbows and his earlobes, it tickled. He was not afraid of drowning, as Frank knew he could float here for an eternity.

I'll have to open my eyes at some point. Although let's enjoy this for a moment longer, it's so peaceful. At this moment, who knows where I am? I could be in a number of pleasant settings, the beach perhaps? No, there is no rhythmic crashing of waves, only a constant pouring. A babbling brook in the forest perhaps? Very serene indeed. There may be fertile woodland all around me, perhaps a family of deer are looking on quizzically at the strange man sleeping in the brook. If I open my eyes and get up, I shall surely startle the deer, and if they flee before I catch a glimpse of them, the argument of their existence would be a pointless endeavour. There is so much tranquillity being gifted to me right now, maybe another five minutes wouldn't hurt... Yes, five more minutes of peace would do no harm to anyone.

Frank tried to lay there for a while longer, however, underneath his eyelids frantic movements and twitching occurred.

But what if I have already been here for another five minutes? And maybe another five more than that... What if I have been laying here all day? It may very well be nightfall when I look around... And if it is evening, then I've lazed through my whole work shift... Maybe even through till the following morning... God what if it's morning? Artemis needs feeding. I may even - depending on how long I have indeed been laying here - be late for my next work shift! What if I get fired for lazing around like I don't have a care in the world? Fuck it, blissful ignorance will have to wait for a bit longer. Get up Frank, Work to do.

Frank slowly opened his eyes and, to begin with, was relieved by the pure daylight breaking through them. He had not been there until night-time. The relief was short lived however, as what initially – through blurred and tired eyes – was assumed to be tree branches reaching overhead, was quickly identified to be interlinking iron and rebar. Everything was so grey. It sprawled across the sky, starting and ending at the horizon, preventing the possibility of any clouds reaching to the ground or, conversely, Frank reaching up to the clouds. A huge ugly cage across the sky with no end that Frank could see, try as he might. His attempts to do so solely consisted of moving his eyes and tilting his head as Frank quickly learned the rest of him was not able to move, *paralysed?* Although he was not in any pain to speak of. As his head tilted back, Frank could see the base of the fountain he was laying in. He could hear the aggressive way it forced water and air out of its top. He could smell the chlorine disperse in the air as the water crashed down, and he could feel the way the water pinned him to the tiled base. Crooked concrete towers, stairways, and plazas invaded the scenery, and once again Frank heard the flapping of wings. *Oh Jesus Christ, not this again.* A mass of birds flocked all around him and began their chattering, head bobbing, and giggling once more as they did with the broken pigeon. *Suppose it's my turn.* The first time Frank was witness to this bizarre event, the pigeon had a broken wing and furiously scrambled around in the water, its talons kicking up, its one working wing slapping the surface of the pool, its head determined to keep above the water, all while being berated and treated with cruelty by its sisters and brothers. Frank, on the other hand, who accepted himself to be the *new pigeon*, simply stared at the birds crowding him. He did not thrash, in fact he could not thrash, his body felt lethargic and was tired of fighting only to inevitably be knocked down again, *why bother, what happens will happen anyway.* He wanted very much to break the habit of thrashing and flapping, and as he remained laying in the shallow pool, he smiled at the thought of his small victory.

The birds began to back away, and for a second Frank felt victorious that he had caused some disruption for his audience, the moment was of course cut short though, *typical,* as from above his head, Frank was greeted by the piercing gaze of two pelicans, whose bills waggled uncomfortably close to Franks eyeballs.

"You again, eh... well where's your friend? There was one more of you last time I was-"

Frank was interrupted by the pressure of two very heavy palmate slapping alternately on each of Frank's shins. The sheer pressure the footsteps applied made him wince, but he didn't dare raise his head as if he attempted any movement the bills of the two birds' overhead would have surely blinded him. He strained his eyes to look down past his nose, chest, and over his belly – *quite the task these days* - to inspect the cause of this sensation. And as much as he hoped it wouldn't be, it was the other pelican. It struggled to keep a sure footing on Frank's soft body, mainly because something very large and – judging by the strained neck of the bird – extremely heavy was concealed in its bill pouch.

"God! No wonder you weigh so much, your beak's full enough to burst! What the hell do you have in there anyway... Oh Christ!"

Frank could see what was in the pouch once the pelican had moved itself onto his midriff. Its bill was agape, and although the pelican's black eyes stared into Frank's, Frank could not help but to stare at the enormous boulder of chalk that was poking out the top of the distended yellow vessel. The strain it had on the pelican was apparent from the translucent quality of the tumescent gular. Veins and sinew were clearly visible from the pale amber pouch.

"How did you even fit that thing in your mouth without breaking your jaw? What do you want from me? Leave me alone all of you! Leave me here in peace! I can lay here forever if I want, to hell with the world and all its apathy! I'd rather wait out eternity here than have another day dealing with the indifference of people and the lethargy it brings me! Leave me be, I said!"

The two pelicans by Frank's head had now moved and pinned each of his shoulders to the base of the fountain by pressing the sides of their heads on his breast, presumably so they could still get a good look at him. The crowd of birds surrounding him began to bob their heads more vigorously and Frank could hear amongst the murmurs and chatter the childish melody of a chant forming 'One, two, three, sphere! One, two, three, sphere!'. The pelicans by his shoulders began to stamp their palmate on the word 'sphere' causing water to splash into Frank's eyes and mouth, he was spitting it out as fast as possible, but it still choked him when the chlorine hit the back of his throat and his eyes were just as wet from the tears the chlorine forced out of him. The chanting grew louder and louder to the point that Frank firmly pushed the back of his skull into the fountain tiling to try to bury his ears under the water and escape the sheer volume of it.

'One, two, three, sphere!'

The pelicans stamped; Frank's ears filled with water.

'One, two, three, sphere!'

The pelicans stamped; the chlorine breached Frank's eardrums.

'One, two, three, sphere!'

The pelican carrying the boulder of chalk craned its head towards the sun.

'ONE, TWO, THREE, SPHERE!'

The bird slammed the boulder into Frank's chest. The impact was so dreadful he could feel his ribs bend and his heart jolt, his lungs deflated underneath the weight of the huge white rock, and his eyes almost popped out of his skull from the pain.

"One, two, three, clear!"

He jolted again, his eye opened wide, and once they had adjusted to the searing fluorescent light above him, he saw

Mr. Neeler and Mr. Lameduc at his shoulders, Kiri above him cradling his head, and a paramedic - defibrillator in hand - exhausted from bringing him back.

"Frank? Frank! He's waking up everybody!" Kiri announced Frank's return to the waking world. "Easy Frank don't move too fast; you've suffered a nasty blow to the head. Here you go Frankie let's sit you up against the wall a bit... There we are, how are you feeling? Headaches? Any pain?"

Frank looked around to see the interior of the mall, he was sat up against a health food shop and a smattering of people had gathered to feign concern for the perfect stranger who had an ice pack pressed to his head. Frank hated the spectacle of the whole thing. He swatted the ice pack out of Kiri's hand and prodded with two fingers at the large swelling around his right temple, he rested his chin on his knees as they tucked into his chest, and he muttered.

"I'm fine, leave me be."

Kiri looked towards Mr. Neeler and Mr. Lameduc, who both shrugged, the latter had noticeably displayed a more energetic cluelessness. Mr. Neeler, being careful to not put his back out – or set off his dodgy hip – knelt to Frank and offered him some water.

"Here you are Frank, you must be parched after all that running around, I'm sure."

Mr. Neeler graciously tilted the bottle for Frank – who found this all very dramatic -- and played his part in *the revival of Mossan*. Seeing this, Mr. Lameduc theatrically sprang to action, Frank saw him dart back over without looking away from the crowd the whole time, *oh no he didn't, oh yes, he did!* The way he saw it, he could not let Mr. Neeler get one up on him. He fumbled around in his pockets and pulled out

97

two biscuits he had saved from his morning tea, they were covered in lint and any signs of a layer of chocolate had long since melted off. Still, they would serve a starving man, at least to prolong the starving and allow that starving man to work and starve another day.

"Hungry, Frank?"

Frank was neither thirsty, nor was he in the mood to chew on the contents of Mr. Lameduc's pockets. However, to spite their *faux generosity*, he took both into his hands and began to consume them. While all this was going on, Kiri, worried that she wasn't doing enough, attempted to console Frank.

"Rest there for as long as you need, Frank."

She saw how uncomfortable the crowd of gawking spectators was making Frank and stood up straight to address them.

"Carry on with your business everybody, this is all under control. Please give this man some space, he has been attacked and may very well have a concussion. The paramedic is here to check on him and his colleagues are here to look after him, it's all under control, please carry on with your days and leave us be."

After hearing this, only one or two of the people actually left - *the angels share* - the rest of the crowd looked over their shoulders to other members of the crowd to see if leaving is what everybody should do. Nobody was giving an answer, just shrugging and asking the same questions, the majority of the crowd remained where it was. Somewhere from the back came a man's voice.

"Who, or what, attacked him exactly?"

Kiri stood on her tiptoes to try to see them man to no avail, then proceeded to address the crowd as a whole.

"A thief, who stole from my cart."

She tugged at her apron, signalling to the 'Kiri's Coffee' logo embroidered across it. More murmurings and chatter came out of the crowd until finally the man's voice spoke again.

"A thief? A thief stealing... coffee?"

Kiri began to explain that the thief had taken money from her cash register, but before she could reach the word 'cash' in her explanation the man rudely interrupted her.

"You're telling me that a thief, lowly enough to be nicking a couple of coffees from a little cart in a mall, managed to not only get away with it but also knocked our chief of security flat on his behind!? What a joke! How can we rely on the security in this place if they can't even stop some little knee-high knob 'ed scarpering off with a couple of drinks?"

Again, Kiri began to speak to try to correct the man and tell him that the thief had stolen money from the cash register and that it was not a child, but rather a very large adult. This explanation, however, could not be heard against the commotion that was waxing among the crowd. The more the man spoke out of turn, adding in false details, the more the crowd bolstered his platform with choruses of 'He's right', 'Yeah' and the odd 'You should be ashamed'. Kiri had completely lost the attention of the crowd and looked towards Mr. Lameduc to intervene. He stepped forward and tried to calm the crowd.

"People, people... Now clearly you are all very upset by this incident, and I can tell that tensions are high, but you must listen to me. This sort of thing is very out of the ordinary. Scenarios such as this do not happen every day and when they do happen our security team is trained to make quick and informed decisions in those moments-"

"Informed decisions?" Another shopper interjected "Your superior's been knocked out by a little boy holding hot coffee! What quick and informed decision was made for that to happen! Don't stand there and lie to us!"

Mr. Lameduc, after experiencing the treatment of the crowd, regained his train of thought.

"Now, now. Let's keep this constructive. The facts as we know them are that a criminal has operated in the mall and our most senior member of security has been viciously attacked. As for the description and the motives of the criminal, I cannot comment, as I was not on the scene when this happened. However, trust me when I say, a full investigation will take place by centralised management to discover what exactly did-"

"Bollocks! Centralised management, pah! They couldn't give a toss, you must be joking, pull the other one, mate!"

The crowd jeered and booed Mr. Lameduc and he looked over to his competitor who was still kneeling by Frank trying to force water into the prone man. Mr. Neeler looked to his colleague, gave a sigh and walked up beside Mr. Lameduc. He put his hands in the air, palms open towards the crowd, then clenched his fists lightening quick, the crowd immediately fell silent and waited for the commanding presence to speak.

"Ladies, gentlemen, we're all brothers and sisters here. I, too, have my problems with the centralised management here in the mall, but rest assured that the landlord has a plan, I will talk with him and-"

Mr. Neeler was also quickly cut off by another wound-up voice in the crowd.

"The landlord!? They're getting the landlord involved now! What's he got to do with any of this?"

Frank heard all the *slander* evolving from the crowd against him and grew so angry with them that he could barely feel his pains anymore, just the burning sensation in his chest. *How dare they?* He thought, *I don't owe them anything, not a bloody thing, and they have the audacity to drag my reputation through the mud. Just after I've been attacked no less!* His thoughts spiralled with every word the crowd was throwing out and he got so furious he couldn't contain his frustration any longer. He bellowed.

"The lot of you! Shut your stupid bloody mouths!"

Some gasps came from the crowd. Others continued jibber-jabbering amongst themselves.

"I've had quite enough of this nonsense; you all stand there with the correct answers, do you? Well, why aren't you off protecting something?"

Ah, I've got them now, the ungrateful fools. He went on to give them a piece of his mind and decided it would have more impact if he were at their level. He stood to his feet - against the orders of the paramedic, and expectedly, began to feel very dizzy and heavy. He stretched out a finger to the crowd and managed to shout out 'Hypocrites!' before dropping back to the floor. Kiri and Frank's colleagues rushed back to his side, attempting to soften his fall by placing their hands under his head and shoulders.

"Easy, Frankie... Easy."

Kiri said. It was the last thing *Frankie* heard before his vision went black once more, and his hearing was taken over by a strong ringing in his ears.

He laid in the blackness for a while. There was no light to illuminate the backs of his eyelids, so he kept them closed. No sound could be heard, not even his own heartbeat, nor the long exhales he was letting out. There was nothing for him to feel, no textures at the tips of his fingers, no firmness or softness of whatever he was lying on, no heat to make him perspire, and no cold to raise the hairs on his arms. There were no scents, not even the familiarity of his own body odour, for a moment he missed it, but it shortly passed. The atmosphere around him did not move, nor was it still, it simply was not. He found it curious that among all this emptiness, one would expect and assume that a person would yearn for the things which filled the world. The colours, the sounds, the smells. These memories would be expected to come naturally to somebody with the aim of comforting their owner. But when Frank tried to recall them fondly - as he felt a person in such a position should if they wanted to, *stop themselves going loopy* – he could only recall the venom which accompanied these sensations. The colours which ceaselessly clashed, all either so vibrant that his eyes strained trying to see them in their garishness, or so dull and muted that they all merged into a grey and brown mire. He tried to recall the noises which would usually bring a smile to his face, he tried to recall birdsong, waves crashing, a fire crackling. Try as he did, all he could remember were the inane chattering of crowds, horns in rush hour traffic, emergency sirens, and mechanical grindings. The only smells that came to his mind were of burning tarmac and acid rain, he wanted so badly to manifest the aroma of his kitchen on Sunday afternoons, where he and his wife used to bake fresh bread, but it was hopeless.

"Get up Frank, Work to do." He heard a voice say.

"Sarah?"

This time Frank refused to open his eyes, for he knew what would happen if he did.

"Pah!" Frank continued with his eyes belligerently shut. "Work to do indeed! The work of a fool who once thought he could be valued for wanting to protect people. The idiocy! To think there once was a time where I would have put myself in harm's way for another, for that ungrateful mass. What are they offering in return asides from further demands from entitled mouths? Work to do indeed..."

Frank remained laying and, keeping his eyes closed, crossed his arms over his chest. He stayed there for a while in silence, until Sarah's voice came to him once more.

"Who is this silly man laying down, sulking like a child? This is not my husband, that's for sure. My husband would never dare to act so selfishly, I know he is a good man. Who are you, are you a body-snatcher?"

"It's still me, people change Sarah. And you know people change for the worse most of the time. I'm no better than that. Changing for the worse. I'm slower than I used to be, I'm certainly weaker than I used to be, I'm of no use to anyone. You saw how quickly I hit the floor after I got hit, I'm past my prime, love. A decrepit old fool who still plays the knight in shining armour for ungrateful louts parting with their money for trinkets. And anyway, why not? Why shouldn't I change for the worse? That's the way the world is going after all isn't it? The 'don't give a shit' attitude is here and it's here to stay. Which is more than I can say for you, Sarah. You left me out in this cold world, and you expect the fire in my belly to rage on? What for? You're gone, and the frost is creeping up my toes."

"Do you not think about starting another fire? One which could fend off the frostbite? Maybe if you could warm your toes, your old feet could run faster, how about that? Maybe if you stopped extinguishing your flame with hot, bitter, black water you could be stronger. Does that sound like something agreeable to you?"

Frank paused for a moment before answering, he wanted to be sure that he had fully considered what Sarah had to say before answering her. He knew his wife, *major smart-arse is Sarah, always catching me out with something*, and in these arguments, he had to think five steps ahead – although even with solid tactics he'd still lose most of the time.

"And what would I do with my newfound strength and speed? Protect you? You no longer need protection. I couldn't even protect you before, let alone after. It's my fault you're gone and if I had more power, I'd only cause more grief. Best I stay here forever, where there is nothing for me to ruin. I'll stay here and argue about how much of a fool I am with you with my eyes closed for eternity, it's a damn sight better than anything that could be had out there."

"You can't stay here Frank; this is no place for the living."

"I know, that's what's so appealing about it."

"And if you do stay here? Who will find Ida, eh?"

"Sarah, there are far more capable people than me who could find that girl."

"But will they, Frank? Will they find her?"

Frank ignored this last part, as he could not answer it without lying, and he did not want to lie to Sarah. Frank remained in place and stopped talking. He was silent and held his breath, he waited at first to fall unconscious, as he did with his previous attempt a few weeks ago in the bath, *bit of an impulsive moment that one.* A minute or so must had passed and Frank could still not feel any light-headedness or drowsiness so he waited even longer, hoping he would soon be able to stay in this world with Sarah. A few more minutes must have passed and still no wooziness to speak of.

Jesus Christ. He thought to himself. *Even something so pure as dying is difficult in this existence.*

He thought perhaps there may be something nearby he could use to speed this up, a rope, a knife, maybe even just a jagged stone he could swallow. However, Frank knew this would mean opening his eyes. He thought about this for a while.

Well maybe if I keep holding my breath, nothing can wake me, at the very worst perhaps I will just stay here holding my breath forever. God knows I'm not dying without at least trying something else... Yes, I'll hold my breath the whole time I look around, just until I can find something that'll finish the job.

Frank opened his eyes, but he only knew he had done so because of the sensation of the muscle memory he had from blinking however many millions of times he had in his life. It was just as pitch black as when his eyes were closed, and there was nothing around, above, or below him. His mouth was tightly shut, and his hand covered his nostrils.

Well, at least it's quiet here. He reasoned. *There are no people dirtying the place up, and it's eerily cosy. Maybe I could just stay here forever. In the serene darkness, the silence of it all.*

For a moment, he thought he heard waves crashing.

Surely not... A sea? Or at least a body of water. All I need is a couple of inches of depth, and I can guarantee a permanent position here!

He heard the waves crash again. He felt a gentle moisture in the air.

It's coming from over there.

Frank started to run – assumedly, towards the sound of the water. It crashed again, much louder this time, and he felt the sea spray refresh his face.

This is it; this is my final goodbye. So long world, you always were a shitty place.

He picked up his pace and started triumphantly sprinting towards the sound of the waves crashing. The sound echoed once more, this time it was surrounding him, it was so loud it bowled him over. The sea smacked him in the face and his eyes instinctively shut to keep the salt water out. He wiped his face with his hands and eagerly opened his eyes with the hopes of another wave finally sweeping him under. But once again, he could feel the familiar sensation of the moon pressing against his back.

No, please just let me go.

It wouldn't. It pushed him upwards out of the only audible waves. It pushed so hard it felt like his shoulder blades would give way. It pushed him upwards at such a velocity he began to feel the air rush past his fingertips once more and his stomach turned as he was rocketed upwards into a flash of light, and it crashed into him as a wave might.

When his eyes opened, he saw *Hadrian's Lino* once again, then the rest of the office came into focus, lastly Mr. Neeler apparated besides him. Mr. Neeler was holding an empty glass.

"Terribly sorry sir, but I didn't know of another way to wake you up, cold water to the face usually does the trick with my drinking buddies. How are you feeling sir?" Mr. Lameduc came over when he heard Mr. Neeler speak, and both looked to Frank for an answer. Frank kept his eyes on the office floor, and a stony expression marked his face. Mr. Lameduc - wanting so badly to break the silence – offered Frank a cigarette.

"Fancy a smoke, Frank? Take the edge off a bit, eh? Here you are... let me light it for you, boss." *Click, click* "Quite a day you've had eh, sir?"

Frank took a long drag on Lameduc's discount cigarette, *tastes like ash before its even lit*, and kept his eyes fixed on the detailing in the floor, as if it was some great equation which needed solving. Mr. Neeler - not wanting to be outdone by his colleague in his boss's hour of need - reached into his blazer and pulled out a hipflask full of gin. He poured it into the empty water glass he was holding and offered it to Frank.

"Bit of Dutch courage, sir?"

Frank wasn't paying attention to what either of the men had to say and at first thought the glass still contained water. He took a sip, sputtered a little bit from the realisation of what he was drinking, then eagerly finished the glass off.

"I dare say you've earned that sir!" Mr. Neeler continued "Whatever is this world coming to, I mean really, thieves striking down good men in broad daylight, absolutely vile. It's a good thing the landlord found you when he did."

Mr. Lameduc furrowed his brow and screwed his face up quite dramatically.

"The landlord? I thought Kiri was the one who found Frank? I didn't see the landlord anywhere, I saw the rest of us doing our best and getting berated by a bunch of idiots, but I didn't see the landlord."

"Well of course you didn't see the landlord, you were probably too busy tracing Kiri's figure or thinking about which watch you want to get from the jewellery store-"

The mention of the jewellery store planted an idea into Frank's mind, but he let Mr. Neeler go on for a bit – *as he's one to do* – so he could formulate some words to convince the two security guards that he had recovered enough to be left alone. He also didn't want an exclamation of *Aha! The jewellery store*! to give Mr. Neeler credit of an idea which Frank was certain he would have come to on his own eventually.

"-but there are other things besides carnal wants to busy yourself with in this world Mr. Lameduc. I saw the Landlord there with my very own eyes. Frank was lying on the floor, beaten and bloody, and the Landlord comforted him, sat him up, and called Kiri over to help. If it weren't for the Landlord, who knows what state Frank would be in now. But, because of this intervention, Frank is almost fully stable, isn't that right, Sir?"

Mr. Neeler had finished quicker than Frank had anticipated, *usually the fucker rants on and bloody on*, and improvisation was called for.

"Yes, that's right. I feel fine... really. Honestly, I should get up and get back to it really, work to do and all that." Frank dusted himself off as he stood up. "Anyway, I've got a couple of things I need to see to, I'll check with you both again before the end of your shifts."

Frank finished off his cigarette and nonchalantly headed to the door.

"Where are you going, sir?"

Frank almost snapped back at Mr. Lameduc *None of your business you nosey, worthless, dogsbody.* But of course, that would be too suspicious.

"Where am I... What? Sorry?"

"I asked where you were going, Sir."

"Oh! Yes well, I'm..." Frank couldn't think of a decent lie, *stupid old fool!* "I'm going to the jewellery store... I just need to ask him a few things about that little girl. I got the impression from Miss Jupeau that Mr. Swinnart may have seen her when he was visiting the sweet shop earlier."

"Oh! So that's where he was! I thought he was just running late. We'll come with you then, Mr. Neeler owes me a watch anyway."

Frank stared at Mr. Lameduc for an uncomfortable moment, he stared directly into the man's pupils and began to breathe quite heavily. His jaw wiggled from side to side to alleviate some of the tension that it was carrying, and his nostrils flared wide. Then, he took a long breath in and replied.

"...Very well then... Let's go."

9

The three security guards schlepped along the intersecting balconies of the upper floor. Mr. Lameduc was trotting ahead while Frank and Neeler dragged their feet a little. The upper floor's network of suspended walkways allowed the mall to impose further distractions and advertisements to its visitors. Whenever Frank was in this section, he was always reminded of his childhood pet, Hammy, and the plastic tubing which created knotted circles around Hammy's cage. He remembered how often Hammy used to get stuck in the tubes, and how one night Hammy had *really wedged himself in there.* So much so in fact that when young Frankie went to free him in the morning, he was stiff as a board and freezing cold, *poor old Hammy.* The security officers walked past the well-dressed shop windows, cafes, bistros, newsstands, and novelty kiosks, each with imposing declarations of 'sale now on!' and 'everything must go!' in very loud colours. Frank wondered as he stared at his scuffed shoes *if someone accepted fault in their own susceptibility and in turn decided to keep their nose pointed at their shoes as they passed along the walkways, I bet the adverts would still get into their mind.* Even if someone did indeed spend the whole time inspecting their laces, the transparent acrylic sheets of the bridging pathways made sure the individual would still be struck with subconsciously planted wants. Since his *run in* with the thief which Frank imagined couldn't have been that long ago, *how long was I out for?* Frank felt so agitated by his self-perceived failure that he felt as though eyes were set in every wall, floor, and window. *Smile! You're on CCTV!* They were staring at him, and only him, anticipating his next move, deciding if it would be something agreeable or reprimandable. However, even with this embarrassment-driven paranoia, Frank no longer cared whether or not his future actions were coherent with the consensus of public morality. He knew that *the eyes* had already made their verdict before Frank even knew what his next actions would be. Suddenly, his stomach felt hot, and he drew in a lengthy cold breath to extinguish it. His head raised as if the air above the average height of a person was somehow fresher than that which everybody else had breathed and he saw the sun dial set in the ceiling once again. He saw the moon's glow through its panes of glass and his back ached and creaked as the *three muppeteers* walked on. As they ambled to the jeweller's, Frank chewed his nails like a man in withdrawal as he put up with his colleagues' inane chatter.

"I wonder what Mr. Swinnart was doing at the sweet shop earlier."

Mr. Lameduc pondered out loud with a slightly furrowed brow, he was taking this thought very seriously, as though he had a formal investigation into Mr. Swinnart's private affairs. It took a short while before Mr. Neeler decided it would be better to talk to his peer rather than conform to the awkward silence which Frank was clearly trying to sustain.

"Perhaps he was buying a present for his child?"

"He doesn't have a child, Neeler. He's not even married; he just sits around his dusty jewellery shop all day pining about the newlyweds that come in for ring adjustments and such."

"Perhaps it was for a niece or nephew then."

"Nope, impossible, he's an only child. I imagine if he did have any siblings his father would have rather handed the jewellery shop over to them instead of Mr. Swinnart. He's a nice enough fellow but a bit of a wet blanket really. A bit of a pushover so I've heard."

Mr. Neeler rolled his eyes and continued to indulge Mr. Lameduc's twittering-on.

"You seem to know a lot about this man, Mr. Lameduc. Who's told you he's a pushover? Do you have your own set of spies running around the shopping centre, gathering information on who you can and cannot barter with?"

Mr. Neeler laughed in a subtly pompous fashion – *he sounds like a horse whinnying* - at the very thought of Mr. Lameduc even being able to manage and pull off something as delicate as espionage.

"Don't be foolish Neeler, of course not... And furthermore, there's certainly no proof leading anyone to believe such a secret group exists. No, get that nonsense out of your head. It's just that I've heard it often enough when I'm within earshot of patrons of the mall, they'll be discussing things about the stores and the owners. Whenever I hear them say 'Swinnart' my ears prick up. They usually follow it up with something like 'Oh, you can talk him down from any price. Not like his father, stubborn so and so'."

"Well, so what if he is a little more lenient with the prices? What business is that of yours anyway? And what does that have to do with him being in a sweet shop this morning?"

Frank had now met Lameduc's trot and raised him a canter. He was out in front of the other two men to try to get them to pick up the pace a little. He had finished chewing his nails and had now moved on to cracking his knuckles and muttering to himself. His right index finger passed over his gold wedding band and the cold sensation of the metal briefly tricked him into thinking he had cut his finger on something. He looked at the ring, rotated it on his finger a few times and made sure Neeler and Lameduc were engrossed in their conversation. He sighed and muttered to himself.

"I don't deserve this. I don't deserve any of this."

The ring was swiftly taken off and put in his pocket. Mr. Lameduc had taken a couple of seconds to think about the question asked by Mr. Neeler.

"Well, I'm not sure exactly why he was in the sweet shop. But the infirm grip that young man has on his prices must be taking its toll on the business. Which is exactly *why* it is of my concern, Neeler. That business isn't going to last long the way it's carrying on, and the shop owner is the bartering equivalent of a pacifist. That means I have a window of opportunity sometime between now and the shop's inevitable liquidation to barter down some high-value items to be sold at cost to me, which I could then sell for my own tidy profit."

"Wipe the drool from your mouth, Lameduc, your true nature is peeking and I must say it's rather unbecoming. Can you really tell me that you would have no problem profiteering at the expense of a family run business going down the pan? What about the legacy of those people? Do you not think that Mr. Swinnart's father may have handed him the business in the hopes that one day it would then be handed to his future grandchild? Your greasy little plan costs more than just money alone."

"It's just the cost of doing business, Neeler. Risk is just as much of an encumbrance to business owners as loans, licenses, taxes, and the rest. It's all just part of the dance we dance. And business owners know that and as well they should. If it were job security they desired they could just go and work for central management and not worry."
Mr. Neeler's hands flapped up in the air.

"There you go again touting central management as the solution to every problem! Have you not considered that perhaps, even with all the loans, and licenses, and taxes, and greedy opportunistic swindlers looking to pick at their business's corpse."
Mr. Lameduc poked his nose in the air and *screwed his face up* at Mr. Neeler's comment, which was nothing more than a thinly-veiled dressing down reminiscent of one a headteacher would deliver.

"Have you not considered, Lameduc, that these people prefer all that peril, anxiety, and uncertainty over the simple shackles which come with dependency? Especially from your deified centralised management, which would only continue to temper those shackles once they were fitted. Some people just want to live at more of a distance from that much order. Some people, although they have accepted that they are essentially trapped within the abstract labyrinth which has been created, would like that labyrinth's pathway to be as wide and spacious as possible. Perhaps they would like to carve out their own silly little frontier, albeit one approved by such organisations as your centralised management."

"Oh yes, illusory freedom. How very poetic, Neeler. Honestly what would be the use of having one's head in the sand and claiming to see the stars? This is just the way it is now, Neeler. And I dare say it's far more efficient than the system which was in place when the landlord was in charge of the mall."

"You take that back."

"I will not. Do you remember what it was actually like back then? Or are your rose-tinted glasses more stained than I thought?"

Mr. Neeler turned away from Lameduc's rebuttal and put some distance between them by catching up with Frank. As he gained second place and matched Frank's gait for joint first, Neeler muttered.

"It was much fairer back then."

Lameduc's *pricked up* ears still heard him.

"Fairer, Neeler!? I suppose it was in the sense that everyone was so equal that *nobody* made any money! Everybody, from the custodians to the shop owners, the security guards to the mall manager, everybody had to go to the landlord with their problems, queries, or requests. Which obviously resulted in such a massive backlog of correspondences for the landlord to go through that none were read at all!"

"That's not true, Lameduc. He may have not been able to respond to many of them but I am sure that he read each and every one of them."

"What ridiculous blind faith you have, old man. At least now with central management things are getting done and shops are finally starting to turn over a profit."

"Even now though, the mall manager still has to answer to the landlord."

"Come on, Neeler. Now you're just clutching at straws, you know as well as I do that that is merely nothing more than a formality. Frank, you remember how bad it was before central management, don't you?"

Frank squeezed the back of his neck and sighed loudly before answering Mr. Lameduc's question.

"Miss Jupeau."

Mr. Lameduc was confused by Frank's response.

"Excuse me, sir? What about Miss Jupeau?"

Frank's neck bent side to side and he felt a little 'crunch' in the vertebrae.

"That's why Mr. Swinnart was at the sweet shop earlier. He had a gift for Miss Jupeau. It was likely more jewellery. Probably his own stock by the sounds of it."

At this moment Mr. Neeler had an *annoyingly audible* epiphany.

"Aha! That explains her rather over-the-top dress sense. Always decorating herself with sparkling tinkery finery! I assumed Mrs. Jupeau's business was just doing very well but all this time it was a budding romance! Nice to hear, eh Frank?"

Frank cut the romanticism which Mr. Neeler had just bloated the air with in his next few words.

"Well from what I gathered from talking with *Miss* Jupeau earlier I don't think the feeling is mutual. Anyway, I'm glad I could help put your sleuthing careers away. We're nearly at the shop now and to be candid with you both I'm still feeling rather agitated. So please keep your typical interference to a minimum. Do <u>not</u> mention Miss Jupeau, I've heard quite enough gossip out of you two to last me a lifetime. I would have happily come here on my own had both of you decided you had anything better to do than to follow around a useless old fool on his personal errands."

"Personal errands, sir? I thought you were asking about the missing girl?"
Frank caught his tongue for a moment.

"...Yes of course I am. But you leave that to me too. The mall manager asked specifically that *I* find the landlord's child. Understood?"
Frank waited for an audible answer to come from behind him. The only sound he heard was the faint rustling of starchy shirt collars as both the men presumably nodded in compliance.

"Good."
Said Frank as he pushed open the mahogany door to 'Swinnart's Jewellers'.

A pleasant bronze bell 'dinged' when the top of the door swung into its clapper as the three men entered.

"Hello?"
Frank called out as they surveyed the interior of the shop. Glass cabinets with dark wooden frames were positioned in such a fashion they created a line of symmetry corridoring the path from the entrance to the cashier's desk. The lighting was dim but not unpleasant as ornate sconces illuminated

the forest green wallpaper. It felt very cosy, and there was a calm warmth to the atmosphere. With all this in mind, the shop did not, however, give off the impression one would expect from a jeweller's. There was an anxious curiosity to the way the décor was set, not the confident grandiosity typically expected from an establishment which dealt in high value luxury items. In fact, were it not for the sign 'Swinnart's Jewellers' above the entrance, one would be forgiven for not realising this was a jewellery shop at all. Due to the fact that on every glass cabinet – of which there were many – the panes had been replaced with frosted glass, and recently by the look of it.

There was an obvious quiet emanating from Mr. Lameduc. He had been talkative and excited on the way to this shop but now they had arrived he was acting as though he had entered a funeral home. Mr. Neeler was busying himself by wiping his finger along the display cabinets and making *equally annoying* audible disapprovals as he rubbed the dust between his fingers. Frank slowly walked towards the cashier's desk with all the mannerisms of a schoolboy in a pub and – while his left hand furtively turned over his wedding band in his pocket – ringed the service bell with his right.

"Lots of bells in here."

Muttered Mr. Lameduc as he pressed his face up to a cabinet to attempt to peer through the frosted glass. Mr. Neeler shushed him curtly as though they were in a library and nodded Mr. Lameduc's attention towards the door behind the cashier's desk. The door led to the back room of the store. It was ajar, and had a faint, flickering candlelight coming from within. The flickering light mimicked the faint, arrhythmic sound of weeping and snivelling from the room.

Frank rolled his eyes, hit the service bell a few times and loudly cleared his throat.

"Ahem."

The sniffing noises immediately stopped, and the screeching of a chair followed, then shuffled footsteps after that, finally the slender figure of a man appeared. He had unkempt blonde hair and a chinstrap to match. For a man so slight, he had strong facial features, piercing blue eyes, a burly jawline - *possibly the result of a slight underbite* - and a rugged nose with a kink in the bridge. His clothes, although understated, were clearly of very high quality. They did not suit his demeanour however; it was as if the clothes were wearing him. The odd way they hung from his body would lead one to assume that somebody had picked them out for him. Curiously, for a jewellery shop owner he wore none of the typical regalia or trinkets, the only decoration that could be seen on his person was a single matchstick, which he had poked through the eyelet in his lapel.

"Excuse me gentlemen. I was making some preparations in the back and did not hear anybody enter. Welcome to Swinnart's Jewellers, how may I assist you?"

Frank replied quickly as not to let either of his colleagues lead the conversation.

"Are you the owner of this shop, sir?"

"Indeed, I am. Edward Swinnart, pleased to meet you."

Mr. Swinnart forced a smile with a closed mouth and looked towards all of the men to wait for a reply from any of them. The corners of his mouth were upturned, but his eyes were filled with repressed tears. Mr. Lameduc, in an attempt to ease the odd tension in the air, spoke first.

"Well, I wouldn't mind browsing some watches while we're here actually-"

Mr. Neeler butted in to stop this from happening.

"Pardon my colleague Mr. Swinnart. He usually has his priorities askew and today is just like any other. He's essentially a child in a sweet shop in your establishment. Which actually brings me to the reason we've visited you today. We're looking fo-"

"Neeler, Lameduc... Have you fixed those monitors in the security office yet?"

Frank didn't even look back over his shoulder as he bellowed the question at his two *inferiors*.

"Excuse me sir? Well... we *were* doing that but then after the events that happened to you earlier, we had to drop it to see to your wellbeing. And then we accompanied you here to-"

"Well, I didn't ask either of you to accompany me here, did I? Look, I'm perfectly fine and capable of carrying out my duties on my own. I think you should go back and finish fixing those bloody monitors. There's no use all three of us doing one task. Leave me be so Mr. Swinnart and I can discuss the matters."

Mr. Neeler was taken aback by Frank's abrupt orders but timidly gestured to Mr. Lameduc that they should leave. Mr. Lameduc's face dropped and he expressed his disagreement.

"But Neeler owes me a watch!"

"That's an order, Lameduc. From your superior no less. Now go about your duties both of you. I will not be forced to raise my voice a second time while we're in Mr. Swinnart's peaceful shop."

Mr. Lameduc flared his nostrils but still nodded, and the two men reluctantly left. Mr. Neeler seemed concerned for

Frank's constitution, while Mr. Lameduc was bitter about his misfortune. As the two men left, Mr. Neeler consoled his colleague by saying they'd come back another time and that he still intended on keeping his promise of a watch. Once Frank felt that he had finally been freed of the burdensome men he apologised to Mr. Swinnart.

"Well, that's no problem, Frank. It must be difficult having to manage people. I know I couldn't do it, that's why it's just me in here. Not that I particularly need any assistance anyway. The shop is never that busy you see."

"I did notice that Mr. Swinnart. I can't help but think it may be useful to have more of your products on display. For example, why on earth are all the cabinets obscured by frosted glass?"

"Please, call me Edward. Or better yet, Ed. It's a good question Frank, and I'll tell you my reasoning. When my father still ran the shop, the cabinets were clear. People would come in regularly, and see the new stock on display. They would see pieces shining in their peripherals and continuously tarry back and forth between items which caught their attention. They would imply things to their significant others, 'Oh honey, wouldn't this necklace look great with that dress you bought me?', 'Sweetheart, these cufflinks would really pair well with your new striped suit.' The kind of suggestive phrases which implants a notion that the jewellery in question somehow always has been a part of that person and that unbeknownst to them until now, owning said jewellery would aid them towards becoming one part closer of a whole identity, which of course will predictably make room for another object somewhere down the line. A never-ending cycle of bolstering an identity which may or may not be false. The other outcome from the clear cabinets was of course a creation of the social obligation to make a purchase under the pressure of the shop owner's presence. My father knew this and exploited it to his benefit with great success. 'Would the lady be interested in the matching earrings to this piece?', 'Perhaps sir would appear a more committed husband with the cufflinks that compliment madame's necklace?' He made a fortune from this shop and his own skills in emotional manipulation. He even made an excess of wealth for him to comfortably retire on."

Frank gave a faux-impressed expression and stated confirmations such as 'good for him' and 'that sounds like the perfect business model'. Mister Swinnart was not upset by these remarks, but clearly had heard these assumptions before. He excitedly continued to guide Frank through his path of reasoning.

"Is that so? And you say this because it makes the most profit? Obviously, a business cannot be sustained without profit, I'm no fool. However, when the shop was handed to me upon my father's retirement I quickly fell ill. There were no symptoms to speak of, but I knew something about this store was the cause of my sickness. I never wanted to be a merchant, you see, I'm more of a creative type, but my father insisted and claimed that the ideal career was something where you could create your wealth quickly enough to grant yourself an early retirement. Unfortunately, the career of an artist grants no such privilege unless one has a great deal of luck bestowed to them alongside their great deal of skill. In fact, it's no secret that most artists make hardly any money their whole career. The majority of fame and fortune comes when an artist has passed away and their work transforms from the profane commentary on the human condition to a sacred lens which magnifies or clarifies the universally shared experience of humanity. The mark of the art is mostly felt once the artist is long gone. My father is too proud of the Swinnart name to allow one of his children to wilt under poverty. Thus, I was given the shop, and because of this, I was growing ill. Eventually – and it took me longer than I am willing to admit – I realised that the colourful precious gems, the gleaming diamonds, the shining silvers and golds which shot from behind the glass cabinets were the very things infecting me. I would spend all day in this shop with these obnoxious baubles showing me pathways which I could not take. The diamond necklaces which open doors to the black-tie events of high society, opera, ballet and such. I could never afford to drown myself with that opulence on my wage. You see, a lot of the profit the business makes still goes to my father. He has in his retirement, taken up many pastimes which have only increased the cost of his living and he is not such a man who would swallow pride and drop his membership to the elite clubs. He would much rather carry on in his self-indulgence and leave me to foot the bill."

Frank wanted to interject and confirm Mr. Swinnart's awareness of how unfair that seemed but Edward did not stop to breathe before moving on to the next item in his list, he seemed to be eternally on the brink of tears and Frank thought it best to allow some catharsis to Mr. Swinnart by at the very least pretending to be interested in what he was saying.

"Then we have the cufflinks..."

Mr. Swinnart continued as he rushed from cabinet to cabinet swaying his arms and presenting each coffin-like container the same way a circus ringmaster would introduce trapezists.

"Symbols of the arbiters of big business. Men who create franchises and fabled legacies among the giants of capitalism. The same men who make snide comments behind my father's back at the events my father is so proud of attending. They look down on him for various superfluous reasons, but the distillation of their hidden animosity is simply that they know just as well as my father does, that he does not belong there. They find his stubbornness amusing and enjoy keeping him close as an entertaining prop, a walking punchline haunting the halls of the country clubs with his head held high from the misplaced pride of his family name. Of course, I have no interest in those people, but the cufflinks give me a constant reminder of their invisible oppression on my father."

Nodding was quickly becoming de rigueur for Frank at this point. Ed continued his homage to the *Cross of Gold,* whether Frank liked it or not.

"Both of those examples are competent enough in explaining why it pained me so much to be looking at these artefacts every day, witnessing people come in and purchase them without so much as squinting at the price. Every now and then I'd get a remark as we finished our transactions 'Oh, you're so and so's son, aren't you?' I was reminded constantly of the fact that although our family in the scope of the general population appeared to be quite well off, there are always parts of society which are cordoned off by illusory walls. Circles within circles which one may attempt to penetrate but never find the middle. People refer to it as climbing a social ladder, but when the areas are walled off as such, one can only get to the top of their own personal ladder to fall off the other side and find themselves locked in a similar paddock as where they had begun their ascent. These thoughts had become very intrusive in my day-to-day affairs and were certainly making me quite ill. But there was one item in the shop which intensified my sickness to a grave level. The engagement rings. The symbols of 'eternal love' and 'sacrifice' which would put a hopeless romantic into serious debt. These items, more often than not, are snapped up by the apathetically wealthy – usually on a whim at their partner's request – as a shallow gesture to comfort their soon-to-be spouse. A token of the relationship they can remind themselves of by looking at it longingly, turning it around their finger on lonely nights while their spouse is away on some business trip, committing infidelity with whomever walks past in a tight outfit. The corruption of a symbol so pure in turn infested my heart with bitterness until I could take it no more. I finally realised that the issue was the glass cabinets. The cabinets did not so much allow browsers to pick out jewellery so much as the jewellery was in fact picking its hosts. And as much as we would infer an engagement ring to be a symbolic representation of our dedication to one another, the fact is that these pieces of crafted metal and stones are completely indifferent to the sentimentality of people. The jewellery itself is an outward representation of wealth, obligatory etiquette, and a corruption of decoration. Those who can afford to adorn themselves as royalty do so without carrying the merit which used to precede it. So, in light of this epiphany, I decided to make the glass opaque."

Mr. Swinnart, with all that off his chest, took a long breath and continued in a calmer manner

"Now, when somebody comes into the shop, the jewellery is not advertising itself to my patrons. It is not imposing any societal pressures of consumerism on the persons and as such they approach me to ask questions. 'Excuse me, sir.' They'd say, 'I want to buy a ring for my fiancé, they prefer silver and their favourite flower is a tulip, do you have anything suitable? 'When the customer voluntarily approaches me with this kind of intimate information, I can find a piece which suits their individual needs. The question I follow with is 'What is your budget?' And because the customer has not seen the prices of any rings yet they can answer me honestly without feeling pressured to inflate what they can actually afford. If I get the feeling that the customer is a genuine and true person and their budget is a little low, sometimes I might alter the price in their favour before showing them pieces which they may like. If I sell at a bit of a loss, who am I to care? The money only funnels up to my father and his ludicrous appearances, let my father's country club rot for all I care. I never wanted to be a jewellery salesman. But at least I am doing my best to keep genuine emotion alive, much like a portrait painter, or a composer, my primary concern is authenticity."

After hearing Mr. Swinnart's unsolicited monologue, Frank felt his sharp edges dull a little. When Edward first started to speak, Frank wanted badly to interrupt with something like 'look, I'm not here to listen to you justify your silly little life, I'm just here to sell my wedding ring which I am no longer worthy to wear in my late wife's honour.' but after listening to him he felt that he may need to approach the subject more delicately, or the sale surely would not happen.

"So, you could say that the main reason for the obscured glass is to quash societal and cultural pressures?"

"Yes, Frank, I would say so."

"Do you like dogs, Mr. Swinnart?"

Edward seemed confused about the question, but eager to find out if it was at all related, so he answered.

"Yes, I like dogs. As much as the next person."

"Well, I have a dog at home called Artemis. Old girl, very sweet, lovely sand-coloured fur and always happy to see me. I do my best to take good care of Artemis and anything she wants from me – providing it is not detrimental to her health – I give to her. Because of this relationship we have, Artemis has gone from being dependent on me for food and water, to expectant of my continued fair treatment to her. At this point she expects me to keep a roof over our heads, and I believe she expects me, albeit subconsciously, to keep her in the best health possible, especially for a dog of her age. Because of this treatment of her she has begun to anticipate her regular walks. This is all part of the deal of our relationship. Now, Mr. Swinnart, what reaction do you think Artemis would have if I gave her away suddenly?"

Mr. Swinnart, who already held the aura of a highly romantic and melancholic fellow, raised his eyebrows and dropped his jaw at this question.

"I assume your dog would be very upset if you were to do that."

"Well, I would like to think you'd be correct in that assumption, Mr. Swinnart. Although who knows what goes on in the minds of our pets. There is so much projection from the owners onto their personalities that really when one looks at somebodies' pet, they are only seeing an egoic illusion of the owner. And this in itself creates no conflict for the animal as they have no narcissism within themselves,

127

they simply 'are'. However, let's presume that my giving Artemis away would draw an emotive response from her. Now, hypothetically, if I let my responsibilities slip somehow. Let's say I am no longer able to take her for walks because I am bed-ridden with some foul illness - perhaps similar to the one you experienced in this shop. Perhaps, because of my immobility and sickness, I am not only unable to exercise my pet but I am also no longer able to feed my dog, or look after it's health. What response would we likely project onto Artemis if I were to give her away to new owners in that situation?"

Mr. Swinnart's eyebrows had now returned to their natural place, and even furrowed slightly as he tried to divine where this conversation was going.

"I think your dog would still be sad, but ultimately you would be doing the right thing."

"Yes... I agree, Mr. Swinnart."

Frank fumbled around in his pocket, placed his wedding ring on the counter with a sharp 'clack', then pushed it towards Mr. Swinnart's side. Mr. Swinnart kept his arms firmly by his sides and barely moved as he stared at the object before him. He turned white as though he had been presented with a dead body, and could not think of a response.

"I'm sorry if I've shocked you Edward, truly I am. However, I would very much like to sell you this ring. I am not precious about how much money it may be worth; I'll take whatever amount you see fair. I'm sure I can trust you. The sale is just a formality so that, should you want to simply return it to me, there would have been a trade of goods and a receipt to confirm your rightful ownership of it. Now, I imagine what you're thinking is that this ring is just another 'outward representation' as you would put it. But I can assure you that is not the case. I have loved my wife since the day I met her. And I knew then that I would not need any trinkets or baubles to make myself feel whole, as long as I kept her by my side and did right by her. We were married quite quickly and the ring became a symbol of our loyalty to each other, unlike the scenarios you smirked at beforehand, I can assure you ours was genuine. I was not alive before I met Sarah. I was merely floating downstream surrounded only by my own reflection in the water. And I needed nothing more than that reflection, I stared at it endlessly, even when friends and girlfriends came in and out of my life. Some of them let go of me to fight the current and get back to shore, and others floated along faster than I and knew I would only slow them down. Either way, I was so fixated on my own image that I barely noticed them. In fact, I was so engrossed in myself that I did not realise when the stream became a river, nor did I realise that ahead of me was the river mouth, and a vast open ocean, deep, dark, and unknown. I floated into that too, but when I had gone out far enough, the water no longer featured my reflection. The ocean was too filled with creatures and mountains and trenches. It did not have time to concern itself with producing the reflection of one useless gawker. I quickly started to drown, and it was only then that I realised I had no idea how to swim. I was sinking, and the water was so black that it was impossible to determine how far down it went. I was thrashing around to stay above but all I did was sink faster. Then I stopped thrashing, and gave into the undertow. I did not enjoy it, and I certainly feared it, but it was all I knew. All until Sarah's hands plunged themselves into the depths and yanked me out. She pulled me up onto a raft and told me it was up to both of us to keep the thing

129

afloat. And that's exactly what we did for seventeen beautiful years."

Mr. Swinnart, afraid of what the answer might be, was compelled to ask.

"Then what happened?"

Frank looked away from Mr. Swinnart and stared at the blue carpet tiles which covered the shop floor, he counted at least twenty of them before continuing.

"She died, Edward. Car accident... My fault, an'all."

Frank gave a long pause and drew a large breath.

"I've not been the same since then. I'm disorganised, I'm irritable, I'm weak – hell, I got knocked to the floor earlier today by some two-bit thief. Sarah isn't here to see me like this thank God. But if she were, I wouldn't allow her to stay with me. I can't keep my end of our deal anymore, I'm useless. And, since Sarah isn't here to divorce me herself, the least I can do is relinquish her of any connection she may have to this old, pointless fool."

Mr. Swinnart leant over the counter and placed a hand on Frank's shoulder.

"Frank... You're being too hard on yourself. I'm sure she would'n-"

"Don't you dare tell me about my own wife! I've thought long and hard about this, Edward. Please, just let me sell the ring."

Mr. Swinnart stared into Frank's glossed eyes until he could hear waves crashing. He looked around his empty shop. He thought about how many times he had seen counterfeits of love occur in here, how many transactions had happened because of it. He knew Frank's love for Sarah was real, and he saw how something he had always held as sacred had crushed the man before him. He slowly nodded.

"Very well, Frank... I'll need to value the ring in the back. Could you watch the shop for me?"

Frank returned the nod and Mr. Swinnart disappeared behind the door he had once emerged from. Frank once again noticed how deathly quiet the shop was as he moved to Edward's side of the counter, leant on it, and faced the entrance with a half-hearted vigilance.

After a while – and after performing several thorough visual audits of all the stock in Mr. Swinnart's shop – *all accounted for, as far as I can see,* Frank began to wonder how long a valuation on a ring could possibly take.

"Christ, what's keeping him?"

Frank grumbled, although he fully acknowledged that was certainly not an expert, and arguably knew very little about jewellery indeed. He began to mentally run through all of the possible steps that a valuation could possibly have. *Bite the gold a bit. Look at the stone with one of those little telescopic monocle thingies. No.* He thought. *This is taking far too long. Perhaps all that sentimental nonsense has affected his professionality.* Frank hunched over onto the cashier's desk. He heard the squeak of polished leather on rubber soles as he crossed one leg behind the other, *rats racing.* His fingers rapped against the top of his receding hairline – *at least I've still got some, better than Neeler's cul-de-sac* – as he rested his head in his palms, and his elbows on the glass counter. He looked all around him for something to distract or entertain him while he waited but the obscured cabinets and secretive lockboxes couldn't even spark a modicum of curiosity anymore. One of his hands moved from his cheek to the countertop and he raised his fingers to begin an impromptu drum roll. As his chunky fingers dropped to meet the countertop, he heard a loud crashing noise upon contact. At first, Frank hopped away from the counter under the vain assumption that he had somehow broken the glass. A mere second later Frank realised that he recognised the noise; it was the same strange noise that came from the back office just before Mr. Swinnart appeared when the men first entered the shop. Frank looked at the fully intact glass countertop.

"Stupid old fool... Can't stop a common thief in my old age and yet somehow, I suppose I could break a thick pane of glass by simply prodding it! Pah! What a worthless curmudgeon I am... What the hell happened to me?"
Shaking his head, he looked towards the door leading to Mr. Swinnart's office. The light had gone out, but a flickering remained, similar to the one in Mr. Vernme's office attic. Frank tentatively approached and gently knocked on the door three times. *Tap, tap... tap.*

"Mr. Swinnart? Are you alright? Mr. Swinnart?... Do you need a hand?... Ed?"
He pushed the door open with his foot, trying to be as non-startling as possible. Frank had a knack for creeping up on people accidentally. He took one last glance back to the shop floor to make sure there was still nobody on the premises, *coast is clear.* He entered. The source of the flickering was immediately apparent. It was coming from the back of the room, sitting on the floor against the wall. It appeared, from far away, to be a diamond of some kind. Peculiarly, even though the room was now pitch-black inside, the object shimmered, twinkled, and glinted strobes of brilliant white light all over the room. The strobes did not act as one would assume light would however, insomuch as they didn't illuminate any part of the room, it was still perfectly dark.

The strobes were more akin to somebody painting white lines through the air. Frank was, *a deer in headlights* as he witnessed the little thing scumble and cross-hatch these little beams out. Before he could muster the courage to get closer to discern exactly what this *eerie fountain* was, the thing had faded and vanished, and Frank was left alone in the dark again.

"Ed?" Frank whispered. "Did you see that thing? What was it?"

Frank took a step forward.

"Ed?..."

He felt the warmth of another person, as he waded through the darkness. A man's thigh brushed against his shoulder. Frank squirmed and recoiled. Once he had calmed his breathing down, *noisy wheezing old fool*, he noticed a faint creaking noise which kept a steady, calm rhythm. *Largo and piano*. The back of his hand created a *timpani-esque* hit as it knocked into a wooden desktop. Frank scrambled around on the desk - *fortissimo*, feeling for something of use. He could hear himself knocking all sorts of metallic objects to the floor - *hi-hats and chinas,* and eventually heard the unmistakable 'clink' of a metal lighter. He dropped to his knees and picked it up, and with hurried and shaking hands, Frank turned the flint wheel over to create an unusually tall flame which filled the room with an amber glow.

"Oh, you stupid, sentimentalist, tragedian! Oh Christ, what have you done?!"

The flame had exposed the components of the room to Frank. The desk chair lay sideways on the floor, which Frank presumed was the source of the odd crashing sound. Swinging above it was Mr. Swinnart, his belt fastened tight around his neck, his cheeks *purple as grapes,* the sharp buckle pressed viciously against his adam's apple. The notched end of the belt had been crudely and hastily modified presumably with a blade and was looped over a heating pipe in the ceiling.

"Stupid old fool! You actually did it, oh Christ!"

Frank scrambled to get Mr. Swinnart out of the air and onto the floor. He righted the desk chair and put it under Mr. Swinnart's feet as Frank climbed the desk and frantically chewed the remaining strips of leather free. As best as he could Frank gently laid Ed on the floor, but it was too late. His eyes were bulged and stared right through Frank's. His limbs were freezing cold and were already becoming stiff. Frank didn't know what to do and without knowing why, he picked up the phone and called Mr. Vernme. The phone rang and rang, and Frank thought about how many documents and papers his distress was being muffled by. How many more letters, bills, and correspondences had *avalanched* the phone since he visited Mr. Vernme's office that morning? Ring ring, ring ring, ring ring, ring...

"Pah, He'll never pick the fucking thing up."

Frank's meaty hand smacked the phone receiver back down. He unclipped his radio and thought about calling for Lameduc and Neeler, he rotated its little plastic body in his hand for a moment while he pontificated, *on second thoughts...* he put it back. *What shall I do?* Frank thought. *Perhaps there is a contact number for his father in that desk somewhere. He didn't sound like the greatest parent but I'm sure even the most negligent father would come down here right away if this happened to their son... perhaps in this drawer? No... In this book? No... Idiot. Not there either...* Frank rummaged around with a nostalgic sense of duty about him. Simultaneously, he was surprised by the underlying epiphany that Ed's death had not been the end of his worldly life. Although Mr. Swinnart had passed away, he was still having an effect in the living world. Frank was now responsible for contacting next of kin. Once the news had been given there would undoubtedly be a lengthy grieving process. Matters of a funeral would need to be arranged by the family, causing them further strain. And then, of course, there would be the matter of the memories. He would not be forgotten for generations within that family, and at family events, weddings and such, the emptiness that the lack of his presence would bring would be felt stronger than any silly argument or tension that could have been experienced were he still with them. Frank thought about the decades and decades it would take for the fallout of this event to subside within the Swinnart family. He also thought of Sarah, and how he had been affected since the accident. Frank had had thoughts which he could now equate to how Ed must have felt in his own *dreary plaza*. But now he saw the aftermath of the actions caused by those similar thoughts plainly laid out in front of him. Frank now knew – *and in a sense I suppose I always did know* - that this was no way to end pain. The suffering's inertia would carry on careening towards loved ones - only causing the transferal and continuation of said pain.

Frank's head jerked towards the shop floor as he heard the entrance door hit the shop bell.

"Eddy? Are you in here? The doors unlocked."

A woman's voice. Kiri's. Familiar, calm, yet somehow unwelcome to Frank's ears at this time. He rummaged around hurriedly on the desk for his ring, his head darted back and forth in the dim light until he saw a tiny glint come from the desk, *more brush strokes*. His ring, and beside it a photo of a couple which Frank assumed to be Ed's parents. He took both, hoping that the latter would aid him in notifying Ed's family of his death. The woman's voice spoke again.

"Ed, are you back there? I've brought you your coffee."

Frank re-entered the main area of the shop.

"Ed's not here, Kiri."

"Oh? But I always bring him his coffee at this time. He likes to have a black coffee in the afternoon to keep him going."

Kiri set the tray down on the glass counter, the surface of the black coffee rippled a strange pattern, creating a faint white shimmer from the reflection of the lights, *pointillist*.

"Kiri, He's... Well, Ed's..."

"He's what? Spit it out Frank for goodness' sake. Are you back there, Ed?" She leaned to look over Frank's shoulder. "You've got the lights off, silly. That won't do! Out of the way Frank."

Kiri brushed Frank aside and walked into the room. Frank stood motionless as Kiri walked past him into the office awaiting a scream to come from Kiri's direction. No such exclamation occurred. She stayed there for a few seconds and then returned to Frank with the same smile on her face.

"Well, he's finally done it then."

She fiddled with the tray of coffee.

"What do you mean 'finally'? You knew about this?"

"Of course. I know about everyone in here, he was always talking about it, Frank. Whenever I came to give him his coffee the subject of death would come up one way or another. I'm surprised he actually went through with it, frankly."

Frank was appalled at how calm Kiri was. He also noticed a slight change in her appearance. He couldn't put his finger on it, which unsettled Frank as he used to pride himself on being able to notice Sarah's slight changes immediately – *Lovely hair, darling. New shoes? You look beautiful as always* – and he always thought this skill translated to other women. No, this was something less cosmetic. Something most people wouldn't see, but the way Kiri looked at Frank made him feel like a prey animal – *small and naked*. She stared right though him, but not with malice, her eyes just pierced him by their own nature, like he was fleeting, unimportant, yet nutritional.

"Well, what are we going to do, Kiri? I don't know who to call, I tried to find his father's telephone number but all I could find wa-"

"I've got his father's number, Frankie. I'll call him, no need to fret."

"What? Why do *you* have his father's number? And how do you know absolutely everybody?!"

"Oh, will you stop asking me things like that, Frank? It's my business to know everyone who comes in here. I wouldn't be very good at my job if I wasn't keeping tabs on everyone. I've been trying to deliver coffee to Ed's father ever since he was running the shop. He's a very elusive man though, always out at social events acting half his age and twice his wallet size. He's always outrunning me that one. But don't worry, Frank, I'll get hold of him. You're probably quite busy, yes? Why don't you run along now."

Frank was wary of the connotation Kiri's previous words carried. *She'll 'get hold' of his father? What will she do with him then?* Kiri stared expectantly through Frank and nodded him towards the door. He transformed from humble rabbit to terrified vole and he scuttled towards the exit.

"Oh, and Frank?"

"Y- uh. Yes?"

"There's a spare coffee going now. If you want it..."

Kiri held the cup out at arms-length and held Frank's gaze. She began to float towards him, pushing the cup – *or is the cup dragging her?* He was tempted. *Suddenly I'm bloody parched.* Closer it came; he could smell the earthy arabica. Closer it came still; the steam curled up then shot to his nostrils. Even closer still; the pleasant chattering of the china saucer caressed his ear drums. Frank licked his lips; but just before the bone white brim made contact with his *smacking chops*, he saw how very black the coffee was – *black as nothing else.* Not even the reflection of the lights shimmered off it anymore, the liquid swallowed it all, and the liquid would happily swallow Frank. He visualised the glint his ring had in the dark office. The white beams appeared once more and one strobed into Kiri's eyes. She looked confused, and as she shook off the feeling he quickly retracted from the cup.

"Oh, um, no thank you Kiri. If I have that now I'll never sleep tonight!" He punctuated his excuse with a chuckle. "Anyway, I must be off. I've got plenty to do today, as usual."

"Oh yes, the missing girl... Well, she could be anywhere. Perhaps some coffee would give you a bit more speed in finding her? Won't you just have a sip? Just a little taste? For me, Frankie?"

Frank produced a toothless smile, keeping his lips tightly shut. Before he could devise a natural seeming exit, he awkwardly bowed – *why the hell did I bow?!* And hurried himself out of the shop. He wasn't sure where he was going, but he knew he could not stay there for any longer, nothing in that shop would lead him anywhere useful. As he turned to close the door behind him, he briefly saw Kiri pull a key from her pocket, unlock one of the cabinets, and pull out a battered old registry book, caked in dust. She marked something off.

10

Frank leant over the golden handrail of the elevated walkway just outside of the shop and caught his breath for a moment. His heart was racing, and he couldn't shake the feeling that he'd just had a narrow escape. But what he had escaped from was unclear. He saw crowds of frantic shoppers pass under him on the lower level. The way they all rippled in and out of each other's way unnerved him, *souls in the Styx*. Somehow, there was a collective sense of direction to the *schools of fish*, even without the presence of a clear leader, motivation or destination. He began to unconvincingly amble along the faux-palisander laminated mezzanine for fear that Kiri might exit Mr. Swinnart's shop at any moment, *play it cool, Frank*. He passed over balconies and bridges, allowing the many advertisement displays to corral him to and fro. Some continuously scrolled upwards, *conveyor belts of consumption,* while others blinked and flashed in a neon hypnotism – reminding customers of products they forgot they 'needed'. The whole set up reminded Frank of road signs and directions, *'this way for great deals!', 'Stop! Amazing bargains inside!', 'Turn right to become cosmetically indebted!'*. There was a similar set of morbid marine life zipping around on his floor. For a while he followed the flow of the crowd, *blend into the furniture*, he thought. All the while Frank made a conscious effort to lie to himself, and pretended that he was doing some patrol work for his security department. Frank had removed his blazer and folded it under his arm - which obscured his badge. He was now 'undercover', looking for the thief that *floored me earlier*. This self-aggrandising pantomime kept its curtains open as he stuck in the centre of the crowd, passing between the smaller cliques of friends and families so that nobody could tell whether or not he belonged to any of them. Any time the group he was walking alongside began to *side-eye* him he quickly veered to the next small group to sell them on a case of misunderstanding, and that he was supposed to be there - at least in some regard. Feigning conversation among the strangers was another of his *covert tactics*, he laughed when they laughed, he sped up with them when they got excited to reach a specific shop, he slowed down with others who were distracted when passing a window display, seamlessly switching circles of strangers, and so on. He kept this up for what felt like to him a couple of hours, although this fatigue was of experiential duration rather than an inevitability of metronomic standards. The truth was, he had barely kept up his veneer-thin ruse for about twenty minutes. Then he found himself a bit hungry, another 'hour' in and he was *more than a bit hungry*. In fact, when he *pulled into the hard shoulder* to sit at a bench and let the crowd pass him by, he realised he was *absolutely famished.* Never had he felt this hungry before in his life. His hunger gave him a great pain in his stomach, a burning sensation in his heart, and a migraine which clouded his thoughts. Sometimes he kept the odd snack in his blazer

141

pockets and - seeing as now that he had stopped walking, and 'laughing', and *hamming up his part*, he thought he'd check his jacket. His body temperature dropped and he shivered. Frank rubbed his hands together and blew into them a few times before he put his blazer back on. His badge was once again plain to see as he continued to rummage around in his pockets for a snack.

"Oh, come on, there must be something... the one day I don't have anything on me... bloody typical."
He felt a crinkle in one pocket and heard a rustling noise, hoping it would be a chocolate bar or a pack of peanuts. He eagerly yanked the item out, *should've grabbed something at Miss Jupeau's*. As soon as he removed the crinkled paper from his pocket, he remembered what it was. He stared at it for a while, and when he started to fiddle with it, the crumpled-up picture dropped Frank's wedding ring into his palm.

"Ah. Yes."
Frank sighed. He straightened out the picture to have a look at Ed's photo. Back in the shop he had assumed it to be an old wedding photo of Ed's parents and -rather ambitiously - hoped there may be some contact details scribbled on it somewhere. However, now that he was under the harsh fluorescent lighting of the mall, he saw no such scribbles on the photo. He also noticed that the photo was not old, and judging by the fashion of the couple in the picture it would have been taken recently, *very recently*. Some of the features of the background were familiar to him, *countertop, cabinets... frosted glass*. The photograph had in fact been taken inside Swinnart's Jewellers in front of some of the opaque cabinets. Frank presumed Ed would have been behind the camera, he smiled and shook his head.

"Sentimental fools."

Frank was drawn in by the picture. The man was in a smart, black, pinstriped suit with a rose-red tie, flashy cufflinks, and a freshly-gelled haircut. He was on one knee facing his fiancée and was presenting her with a very modest, but very earnest engagement ring. It was clear that the soon-to-be groom's young face – *even with the shaving rash and acne* - was blushing with anticipation and hope for the future he was about to share. His wife-to-be was wearing a long summer dress with a floral print. She had a ribbon in her golden, hay-coloured hair, and held her fingers in front of her mouth. The pose was *blatantly rehearsed* but it wasn't a concrete persona the couple were engaging in, more of a *brittle façade*. It wasn't difficult to *see behind the masks* as the couple were clearly open and genuine about their feelings. Frank could still see the core of the initial, candid excitement the young lady had experienced during their proposal. Her eyes were wide and brimming with ideas of potential roads the couple could blissfully travel down together. He could see the slight wince being partially hidden by the young man's smile, probably due to a pain shooting up his knee, *how many shots did you take, Ed?* All of this was a beautiful thing to see, but that wasn't what made Frank smile. Frank was imagining Mr. Swinnart behind the camera, happily immortalising this moment for the lucky couple. Frank reasoned that Ed probably offered to take the picture, in fact, the picture was probably Ed's idea in the first place. Frank thought about Ed hurriedly scurrying off to fetch his camera and doing what he could to make this day as good as possible for these two people. Frank chuckled at the thought. The notion of seeing Ed happy consumed him. *Perhaps seeing a smile on that morose face would be the thing to bring some closure.* He brought the photo closer to his nose and squinted. Frank thought he could see a reflection of Ed in the window in the background. He looked hard for a moment at the out-of-focus figure – *like a magic eye*, the proportions of the figure suddenly came into view. The figure was not a reflection of Mr. Swinnart: the tragically romantic jeweller. Rather the figure was on the outside of the glass, running past the window. It was a little difficult to make them out, the image was a bit blurry because of the speed they must have been running at. But by looking at this figure for only a second Frank felt a lump in his throat. It was a small figure, a child, and Frank felt it in his gut.

"That's her."

The little girl looked nothing like the varying descriptions Frank had heard from the people he had inquired with that day. They all seemed to have a different idea of what she looked like, what her mannerisms were, even what her physicality was. None of the descriptions given to Frank during the course of the day matched each other and they certainly did not match the little girl Frank was now looking at in this picture. But regardless of this Frank knew it was her. It was a sensation more than just knowing, he *felt* it was her. A part of him that was distinct from everything that Frank thought he was. A part of him that he always knew was there but never needed to remind himself of. A part of himself which was beyond lies or truth, sloth or ambition, knowledge or bliss. The part of him that simply was, and was happening, and will continue to happen after Frank's body became *worm food*. This deepest part of Frank was telling him that this was the missing girl, undoubtedly. What caused more distress to Frank was that in this picture, the majority of the girl's image was blurred as she was running,

144

but her face was sharp as reality, and Frank could see she was screaming. Her expression was *more Munch than Wilhelm*. Terror. It was quite lucky that the girl was in the photograph at all, as if she had been just a bit further into the background, Frank wouldn't have been able to make her out at all and he may have lost her forever.

"That poor thing! Crying out for somebody to find her. I'd of given up, neglected my duty. How could I? How dare I?! This poor little one is out there, scared and alone while I've been moping around and skiving off!"
Frank stood up from the bench, his knees creaked and his back cracked, his hips popped and his heartbeat rose in unison with his *flabby old arse*. He carefully folded the photo and placed it in his top pocket. He shook his head at the floor, *a self-centered old fool*. He placed his wedding band back over the pale indent it had left on his finger, and took a deep breath in.

"Get up old man, work to do... How selfish I've been. One little knock to the head and the only thing that's important to me is my own self-pity. I've been dragging my feet and acting as if the world has done me a disservice. Imagine how swollen my head must have been for me to think the world owed me any courtesy whatsoever. And what part on my end is being offered in this transaction with the world? My continued patronage? As if my leaving this world would cost so much that the rest of the people would follow suit, the animals would surely die, the oceans would dry up, and the earth would spin into oblivion as it no longer had me to revolve around... Twat."
Frank started a clumsy run whilst weaving in and out of the crowds of people who would inexplicably change directions as they pressed their faces against shop windows. His

leather shoes felt tight and his heels were bruised. His knees had a sharp pain from all this unwelcome and uncommon motion but still he carried on.

"I hope those two buffoons have finally got the security monitors working now. If I can see where she ran to from Ed's gaff, I might still have a chance of finding her."

11

Inside the security staff office Mr. Lameduc and Mr. Neeler stood on either side of the security camera control panel. They were acting as though they had drawn a line down the centre of the console and agreed upon their territories the way fighting siblings would in the back of a car. Now the dust had settled and an unspoken treatise was in place, both parties had returned to pouting. Mr. Lameduc was once again filling the room with cheap tobacco smoke as he paced back and forth between the camera screens and the filing cabinets. Mr. Neeler made sure that his expression clearly conveyed that he disapproved of Mr. Lameduc's actions from a distance, yet every time his colleague turned towards the filing cabinets, Mr. Neeler slyly took his hip flask from his breast pocket and took a hasty swig. Both men were interspersing the tense silence with passive-aggressive sighs, and by muttering to themselves. According to the natural etiquette of their passive-aggressive call and response, it was once again Mr. Neeler's turn to mutter something, and he did so right on queue. His timing on this particular coda was so perfect that it inspired Mr. Lameduc to go off sheet and exclaim something a forte.

147

"What did you just say?!"

Mr. Neeler looked up from his crossed arms - which weren't hiding the outline of his hip flask anywhere near as well as he thought – and gladly repeated himself at Mr. Lameduc's request.

"I said, Lameduc; I. Don't. Know. Why. We. Haven't. Fixed. It. Yet... Is that clear enough for you now?"

"Don't start, Neeler. I've explained this to you over an' again now. You're really getting on my last nerve. You *know* I'm waiting to see if those workmen come back with any spare parts that we might need before we rush into anything."

"Rush into anything?? Hah! Rush into anything! Lameduc, we're talking about putting batteries back into a remote control! You're acting as if we're going to install solar panels on the roof in the middle of an earthquake! And, need I remind you dear colleague, that those workmen were nothing but lying children who pulled one over on you. They're not ever coming back, let alone with a bunch of bloody spare parts that would be as much use to you as alien artefacts!"

"See, that there, that's exactly your problem Neeler, you don't trust people. You assume that you're above everyone and that only you hold the right answers. Those 'lying children' as you called them, told me that they're workmen and I believe them because they've given me no reason not to. Unlike you, I actually understand the working man and I'm sure if I had been there for your interaction with them, I would have been able to recognise the blue-collar wit they were pulling over your eyes. God, you're so pompous and ignorant, Neeler. I bet you've never set foot in a working-man's bar, you've never experienced the smell of stale beer on green pool-felt. They're good people, honest people, and there's no reason to treat them otherwise."

"This is entirely out of the blue." Mr. Neeler scoffed, "I never said anything disparaging about working class people, Lameduc. In fact, I'll have you know, I grew up in such a household. I was merely pointing out the fact that you are foolishly waiting in vain for some children who tricked you – quite easily I might add – and that you will never see them again. But all this is beside the point, I'm simply asking you why you haven't put the batteries in the remote controller yet."

"Well, Neeler, it's not as easy as that, is it? There could be a number of reasons unknown to us to why we shouldn't put those batteries in, but we won't know the answers to any of those hypotheticals unless we wait for these workmen to come back with those parts. Some may be relevant, some may not be relevant, but I put my trust in the kind of people who built this country and I will proudly rely on their expertise in this situation as history has shown us to do many times before."

Upon finishing his little speech, Mr. Lameduc looked around the room expecting some smattering of applause, of course there was none as Mr. Neeler was the only other person in the room - and he certainly wasn't going to clap. His 'closing statement' was met with the harsh reality of silence and, disappointed by this, Mr. Lameduc returned to his pacing between the monitors and the filing cabinets. After a few rounds of pacing, Mr. Lameduc asked a very simple question.

"If you're so sure about this, Neeler... Why haven't you put the batteries in the remote yourself?"

Mr. Neeler flapped around and let out a breathy 'well I never!'. He put his nose in the air as if that would get him out of answering this question. Mr. Lameduc asked it again, with a pinch more authority this time.

"Don't evade the question, Neeler. Why haven't you put the batteries in? It's as much your responsibility as it is mine."

Mr. Neeler's eyes rolled, his mouth dropped – which further elongated his face - and he let out a huge sigh before answering.

"And what good would it do for me to put the batteries in? I know very well that the answer to our problem is indeed those batteries but you hold so much doubt over me saying so. So much doubt in fact that were I to fix the problem with a blink of my eyes, without even touching the batteries once, and you witnessed the whole thing and were able to operate the monitors afterwards *because* I had fixed them with this fantastic feat, you *still* wouldn't believe me. If I were to put those batteries in myself you would see that that is the answer, however you would have not learned the answer for yourself, nor would have gained the humility to accept the truth after doing so. I have told you the answer, Lameduc, it is *you* who needs to have faith and carry that answer out."

Mr. Lameduc's head sharply turned towards the door as he heard the footsteps of someone approaching. He flashed a smug grin over to Mr. Neeler which presumably meant 'here come the workmen, you'll look like such a fool once they walk through that door'. The grin quickly vanished however once the figure rushed through the door.

"I need to review the footage for camera six, the one outside the jewellery shop! Quickly!"

"Frank! Where have you been?"

"No time Lameduc, pull up camera six, now!"

There was a dead silence in the room but for once it wasn't because Mr. Lameduc had finished talking. Frank excitedly ruffled his thinning hair and rolled his jacket sleeves up. He approached the desk of the monitoring system and leant on the surface with his palms, looking the whole console over and scanning around for something to happen, his excited smile started to wane. Neither Mr. Neeler, nor Mr. Lameduc had said a word, yet they exchanged glances over Frank's shoulders, *kids in the passenger seats.* A few dead seconds passed in the room without even the dust daring to settle.

"...Why are these screens black?"

The two men desperately tried to explain their reasons and rationalise the inaction which had occurred on both sides. They also tried to make one-another out to be some sort of obstacle which stood in their way of completing this 'gargantuan' feat of replacing the batteries in a remote control. Frank's excited smile faded more the longer the men babbled and, after a short while, it had completely disappeared. He kept his gaze set towards the console, furrowed his brow, and whispered to the two men who were frozen behind him.

"Get out, now."

The men looked at each other. The car was being turned around.

"I'm sorry, sir?"

"You both heard me perfectly well. Get out! Now! I've a right mind to sack the both of you on the spot. It's amazing how two men who are apparently polar opposites can manage to find a middle ground in their complete and utter ineffectiveness. A remarkable phenomenon of reflected

151

ineptitude! All either of you ever do is slow things down to a grinding halt then blame one another and drag me into ridiculous arguments over who was the most useless that given day. Well, I've had enough of it! It's clear to me that neither of you have any intention in carrying out your duties in any capacity, let alone doing so with any amount of efficiency or dignity! You both tell me not to trust the other in this task or that, yet there are ulterior motives hiding in both of you! I've put up with you pair of filibustering dickheads for years and during those years you have etched a rift across me so you can exploit whichever half benefits you the most! Second guessing myself. Warring with myself. Imagine if one day I were to close that rift and use my whole self to make you both completely redundant? Well, it just might be today! Believe me when I tell you I've had enough. And why not this day? There is no day in the calendar plotted out to be any more perfect than any other to take matters into one's own hands and steer my own vessel. Now get out. The both of you!"

The two men looked shocked and puzzled, but in their shock and confusion, both men remained awkwardly stationary. Mr. Lameduc - *pale as a ghost* - *piped up.*

"You can't fire us, Frank. Those sorts of decisions were standardised and handed solely to central management. If you want to file a complaint about us you can do so. Possibly - after enough complaints about the same issue reaches centralised management, of course - you may receive a correspondence which invites you to formally and verbally state your grievances with us. After a few of those the possibility of our termination may be considered by a board of governing directors who will take your complaints - as long the complaints are no older than one year, and there is no cessation between complaints longer than three months – into consideration. But you can't just fire us because we're ineffective at our jobs, Frank."

Mr. Neeler, picking up on his colleague's red tapestry, spun a little of his own.

"Once again, Frank. I agree and disagree with my colleague Mr. Lameduc. He is correct when he says you cannot fire us. But not because of centralised management. The truth is that nobody has the power to fire anybody apart from The Gentleman, Mr. Yharzervay, The Landlord."

Frank finally turned to face the men, and there was an ember crackling in his eyes, waiting to fully ignite.

"Right! Fuck it then! You're both so bloody indispensable the only thing I can do is take myself out of the equation!"

Frank paused for a moment before the fire could fully begin to roar, and composed himself. He took a deep breath in until it felt like his lungs might burst. Usually, Sarah would be around to calm him down. But he no longer heard her voice. In fact, once he inevitably exhaled that long breath, he heard no voices whatsoever. And for once, rather than the familiarity of loneliness, he felt a respite in his self-composition. This sensation surprised him. He had never known that he could hold such a powerful stillness before. The fire in his eyes calmed, he retained the same feeling of strength without the rage which accompanied it so predictably. Frank lowered his voice, and continued.

"First thing tomorrow I shall march into Mr. Vernme's office and quit on the spot. However, until our shifts are finished for the day, I am still your superior. And as your superior, I am giving you a direct order to leave for the rest of the day. You will be paid for the full shift and I

153

will make sure to offer some praise for both of you tomorrow to Mr. Vernme." Frank turned to Mr. Neeler "I will instruct him to also pass this praise on to Mr. Yharzervay." The pair found this proposition most agreeable, and promptly left Frank for the day as he requested. Frank took a few more deep breaths - as he found them to be oddly enjoyable - placed the batteries into the remote control, and began to review the footage of camera six. The machine whirred and flickered as he scanned forward through the early morning hours. Within a matter of seconds, he witnessed the footage of the Swinnart's Jewellers shop front turn from an eerie and empty passageway - which only had rolling dust to create some movement – into a tumultuous rapid boasting furious waves of people which swelled and crashed along the banks of the storefront windows. The sped-up nature of the footage removed the humanity from the way the people moved, *like an Attenborough doc, one with creepy crawlies*. Their actions were jerky and didn't appear to be based on premeditation nor impulse. They acted the way Frank imagined atoms would, bouncing around, almost bumping into one another. Man in its most liquid form. After a while Frank found the movement quite hypnotic and as the blurred appearances of the crowd offered no insight to their personalities - the individuality of the people melted away. Just as Frank was really beginning to find himself transfixed with this phenomenon that only he was witness to, the flow of traffic petered out and he was once again acutely aware of his surroundings, his occupational responsibilities followed shortly after.

"The lull before lunch."
Frank said to himself, somewhat disappointed by the appearance of a quiet period. However, just as the calm

nature of this point in the footage began to lose Frank's interest, he saw two small figures dart past the screen.

"What was that?! Must be her! Agh, go back, blasted thing!" He mashed the buttons on the controller. "No! Back I said... No, not that bloody far... Right, there we are, ok, and play."

Frank watched the footage, and sure enough, there was the girl. He matched her terrified expression up with the photo he had in his pocket. It was her alright, only she looked a little older than he had imagined. Granted, the photo was blurry, but even so, her bone structure held the weight of a teenager, not the freeness of a child. He saw her run past the jewellery shop window. She was clearly screaming and at one point looked over her shoulder. It was at this point that Frank saw exactly what the girl was running from. She was being chased. Not by a kidnapper or malicious attacker, but rather the girl was being hunted down by a figure on all fours. Its mouth was open and drooling, its tongue flapping against its jowls. The most curious thing about this creature was its energy, a clumsy sprint fuelled only by its appetite. However, what surprised Frank about the creature most was that although it appeared warped to how he remembered it, Frank recognised it instantly.

"Wait... That's impossible... Artemis?"

Frank would have recognised his dog anywhere. It didn't matter that in the camera footage Artemis's features had also changed. The majority of her was still covered in greyish-brown, wiry fur. Her torso still kept the same greyhound-like taper. However, her snout had become shorter and wider which allowed for her new, large fangs to creep out from her upper jaw. Her missing eye had been replaced by a large amber one which reflected light straight

155

back into the camera's lens. Her tail had become long and slender, with short, black and orange fur. And in place of her missing foreleg was one covered in the same black and orange fur, the paw of which concealed very large, razor-sharp claws. The new leg seemed to be hindering Artemis somewhat, perhaps she was not used to the way it worked, or maybe it was longer or shorter than the others - but either way Artemis clearly had trouble keeping herself upright on it. Because of this asymmetrical limb, Artemis – although clearly intending to harm the girl – could barely keep up with the fairly average speed the girl was running at. Both of them quickly ran out of frame and Frank hastily flicked through cameras to get a view of them again. He re-joined the commotion when he flicked to camera three, just as they raced through The Birdcage. Perhaps it was the camera angle, but Frank could have sworn the girl looked different now, *Older? No, impossible. Taller maybe?* The girl was having to shove people out of the way as they idly meandered along the route. Even after bumping into the girl, they seemed oblivious to her existence and turned to each other in mutual confusion as though only a strong breeze had moved them. It was only after Artemis - with her new leg and strange new tail - bounded past and knocked over Kiri's coffee cart that any of the shoppers noticed a commotion at all. Again, Frank had to flick through cameras to find them, he did so on camera seven which pointed to the east exit of the mall. The two of them seemed to have changed once again. The girl seemed *taller still* in this shot, and Artemis had more of her body covered in orange and black fur; it was spreading quickly. Artemis chased the girl through the shopping centre, and out of the door. However, Artemis stopped at the threshold and merely watched as the girl ran across the busy road where cars swerved to avoid her, some hitting each other in the panic. Frank watched as the girl sprinted down the street. Once she was out of view, Artemis paced up and down the doorway a few times before she *slinked* into the shop by the east exit. 'Thomas Young's Instruments and Accessories'. The music shop had been there long before Frank started working in the mall, yet he had never introduced himself. The store did fall under the protection of the mall security however, the security guards were never requested to include it in their patrols. Moreover, the owner had never asked for the security guards' aid in any matters. Frank looked at the recorded time in the top right of the screen and saw that this whole commotion had occurred mere minutes ago. He shot out of his chair and bolted out the office door.

12

It wasn't long after Frank had begun running that he became *puffed out.* The loud bang the office door made as Frank slammed it behind him was his starting pistol, but his sprint – *hundred yards, more like* – soon decreased to a power walk, *the kind Mrs. Wainwright does around the cul-de-sac on Sunday mornings in her funny spandex.*

Through his hyperventilation, Frank tried to fool himself.

"The shoes... It must be... The shoes – not trainers... That's the problem."

Each desperate breath he drew in burned at the bottom of his lungs, and his gait became weighted and laborious. When he tried to pick the pace back up, he felt as though he were running in slow motion, or that a piece of elastic had tied him to his point of origin. *At last! Fucking finally!* He thought as he saw the prone coffee cart under The Birdcage a hundred yards ahead. Splintered bits of wood sprawled out in the mire of dark roast coffee beans, spilt milk - *nothing to cry over* - and disposable cups. He attempted a courteous and final sprint as Kiri caught sight of him.

"Frank! There you are! Thank goodness you're here! Look what's happened to my cart! Some beast knocked it over a moment ago, whatever should we do about this?" Frank's palms planted firmly on his knees as he sucked the air into his lungs as hard and long as he could. Once he had stopped seeing stars, *Jerry'd knocked Tom with a rolling pin*, he produced a handkerchief from his pocket and began to wick away sweat from the corners of his widow's peak. He desperately wanted to ignore Kiri's question; *how do you go about explaining this? Oh, yes Kiri a girl and a bloody chimaera just ran through, pretty standard stuff. Back to it folks, nothing to see here.* Unfortunately, Kiri wasn't solely asking on her behalf. A large gaggle of shoppers had gathered around the destroyed coffee cart, and they were all looking to Frank. He recalled the barrage of anger that his last crowd presented him with and felt somehow compelled to put on a show for the crowd of strangers. Deep down he knew that he did not owe these *silly sods* anything and if he wanted to, he could very well ignore the lot of them without any real repercussions, after all, *what are they going to do? Have me fired? I'm off down the jobcentre tomorrow anyway.* Yet, once *all eyes* were on Frank, he felt a cosmic obligation to address them. He straightened himself out, gave a faux-professional, *shit-eating grin* to Kiri, and headed over to the up-turned cart. Kiri returned a similar smile in his direction. However, Frank could see straight through her saccharine expression. He saw her eyes were hungry and hollow, and she clearly knew that had she not drawn the attention of the crowd towards Frank, he would have surely kept running past her.

"Oh my, Kiri. What happened here?" Frank did his best to sound genuinely concerned.

159

"My cart, Frank! It got knocked over by some beast!"
Kiri turned towards the crowd and held her arms open,
fingers spread apart at waist height.

"It's lucky it bounced off one of these poles. Why, it
could have just as easily hit any one of these good people!"
The crowd rippled with gasps and murmurs, Kiri had them
round her little finger, but before she could rile up the crowd
further, Frank interrupted.

"Oh gosh... What do you mean by 'beast', Kiri?"
His half-hearted delivery was not what Kiri had hoped for on
her production's opening night. To make up for her cast
member's lacklustre performance, she strained her
annunciation and projected over the *toupees in the cheap
seats*. Kiri paced up and down in front of the arabica-infused
collateral damage, it served as a dramatic backdrop for her
monologue.

"Good-ness! It was horrrrible, Frank! It had allll sorts
of different fur on it, mottled and hideousss! It had
sharp fangs, piercing eyes, and huuuge claws! Look, it
even clawed at The Birdcage!"
Kiri drew everyone's attention to one of the metal poles of
the huge structure, which had been badly damaged.

"Wow!"
Exclaimed Frank - only this time his reaction was not for the
benefit of the crowd, he was genuinely surprised. He
inspected the damage to the metal pole. The claw marks ran
roughly three lengths of Frank's handspan and were a *good
few inches* wide. His hand kept instinctively pulling itself
back as he felt the jagged torn metal *grating away* at his
fingertips. The gold exterior had been ripped completely
open. It was a much thinner layer of gold than Frank had
expected. The laceration had exposed the material behind

160

the gold veneer, lead piping - which was also agape - housing columns of now-escaping asbestos fibres. Frank was still trying to calm his breathing from his *pitiful excuse for a run*, and because of his deep inhalations, he could feel the dispersing material *scrape away at me windpipe*, his lungs began to feel hard and stiff, *a Papier-mâché'd balloon*. He could feel himself corroding from the inside just from standing close to the *bodge job* shoddy structure. However, he harboured an unusual admiration for the damage which had been inflicted, and before turning back towards Kiri and their *audience*, he thought *Wow... Artemis really did this?*

"You're telling me some animal did this?"

"Not an animal, Frank. A wild monsssterrr did this! It attacked my coffee cart and almost knocked down this whooole golden structure!"

The crowd rippled with more hushed nattering as Frank raised his *stage-side* eyebrow and stared at Kiri for a few seconds - giving the audience a beat to catch up - before replying.

"Right you are, love. And this 'monster', what were its motives? It must have had a reason to cause this mess, eh? For example, was it in distress perhaps? Surely, a wild animal – or 'beast' as per your description - in a place like this would easily feel trapped and unsafe, perhaps it was panicking? Or maybe it was hunger? It could have gone for your coffee cart because it was looking for nourishment, then - after realising that clearly none of the contents within that cart could sustain an animal such as itself - it might have moved on. Or even - if it were indeed hungry – the cart may have just been in the way of what the beast was really hunting down. Did you happen to see it chasing anything Kiri? Or maybe even anyone?"

Kiri's face dropped for a moment, and she realised that she was not the only one putting on an act. Quickly reprising her role as Shocked Victim #1, she feigned to be in thought for a moment and then sweetly replied for the benefit of the audience.

"No, not that I could see, Frank. It just charged through here on all fours."

"Charged through on all fours, I see. And it definitely had four legs, Kiri? Four. Not any less, not anymore? Eight? It wasn't a spider, was it?"

Frank subtly winked, stage-side again, naturally. Kiri's face turned sour; she knew there were no more games to play with Frank. He had seen too much. He had witnessed how she planted seeds at Puerillo's toys. He had experienced first-hand how she nursed the germination of the seeds she had planted in himself, and he had seen her bountiful harvest swaying in the draughty back office of Swinnart's Jewellers. *The eight legs of progress come to swallow me whole.* She had one last resort to use to keep the sheepskin slipping from her back.

"No, only four legs, Frank. But this beast was huuuuge!" She motioned to the crowd once more. "You'd need a good bunch of people to have a chance at capturing the thing! Perhaps your colleagues could help you, Frank? They surely would respect an order from their superior?"

Frank set his gaze to the floor.

"Well, they may have at some point. Perhaps. But..."

"Whatever is the matter, Frank?" Kiri smiled.

"I doubt they'd follow my orders anymore. I won't be their superior for much longer. I told them of my intentions to quit tomorrow morning."

The crown rumbled with chatter again, shaking their heads and tutting in their disapproval. Kiri – who was really putting on a pantomime at this point, *My, Kiri! What big teeth you have!* – faced the crowd and widened her eyes.

"What?! Frank! You're quitting? You would do that so easssily? Giving up your rrresponsibility of protecting these fi-ine people, no less! Do you not care for them anymorrre?" Frank continued to inspect the floor, shuffling some of the milky beans with the tip of his shoe. His heart sank, his stomach rose, and a hollow stone was lodged between them. Kiri continued.

"Well maybe it's for the best. There's no way a man as unrrreliable as you would be able to catch this beast anyhow. No, best to leave it to somebody more motivated, more ambitious, more conscientious, strongerrr, youngerrr, healthierrr."

The crowd were responding in agreement with *Judy's* beratement of *Punch*. So much so that the noise of The Birdcage's columns was relatively masked. Nobody, apart from Kiri, had noticed the swaying of the golden poles up until now. She thought not to share the information that the poles were creaking - and inevitably toppling. *Dozens of birds with one stone.* The whole thing had been creaking like an old birch since the animal had gouged a chunk out of one of the supports but soon enough, everyone in the mall was aware of the danger. The pole which was damaged by the animal slammed into the floor - narrowly missing Frank's head – and let out a cacophonous bell-like resonance, the pitch of which caused the crowd to cover their ears, some of the more elderly members dropping to their knees. The other columns began to fall in a domino fashion, some of which landed on panicking shoppers, crushing them under the weight – *ding, dong, thud, ding, dong, squelch.* Frank had instinctually dropped to the floor and began crawling out of harm's way. He got clear of the immediate danger, scrambled back to his feet and instructed the crowd to disperse.

"Everybody! Exit the premises immediately! Fire exits are clearly marked! Head out your nearest one!" Some of the crowd – those which heard him over the metallic commotion - listened to Frank, others continued to panic. A few of the calmer people tried to relay the message to help as many people get out as possible. Others were helping seniors back to their feet before effectively dragging them from the impact zone. Over the clanging and the clatter of destruction, the cries and screams were scantily heard. Some of these self-appointed ushers were grabbed at the sleeves and ankles by people who were immobilised by their own fear. They held onto the ushers vehemently, despite the attempts to have them shaken off. One such usher had a man at their ankle and a woman tugging on their coat.

"Stop tugging at my clothes! Get up! You're going to get us all killed!"
They tried to shake loose but to no avail, even when their arms freed themselves of the coat sleeves the man and woman gripped their forearms and held onto them for dear life, pulling them in opposite directions and anchoring them on the spot, sealing the fate for all three of them as the last column crashed down upon them. It bounced off the marble floor just enough for Frank to see three mangled bodies underneath it, before promptly landing on top of them once more, obscuring their crushed torsos for good. Kiri stood in the middle of the destroyed area, not a scratch on her, patiently staring at Frank, who was still in shock, and his

ears still ringing. Kiri's voice gradually began to fade in on top of the piercing ringing.

"This is your fault, Frank." She said calmly. "You're giving up your position as head of security and now look at what's happened. All these people. All this mess. All because you don't want to deal with this anymore."

Frank's eyes darted around his head trying to process what he had just seen. *I'd kill for a gasper right now*, he thought as his fingers fiddled around in his pocket linings, hoping to find one – *and a lighter to boot.*

"That's not true."

Frank replied. This response surprised Kiri somewhat, she was expecting a timbre of defeat in his voice, but there was a surprising amount of rationality backing up his statement.

"This is not connected to my responsibilities, and you know it. If you must lay blame to someone, look elsewhere. I saw what happened to your cart on the security monitors, Kiri. It wasn't a monsterrrrrrr; it was an animal. An unexpected event, yes, but what sort of manmade structure cannot withstand an attack from an animal? Truly shoddy. What use are all our decoration, decadence, and feigned transcendence from the animal kingdom if all we do with it is create a cage? And a cage that can be crumbled by the slightest interference of an animal no less?"

"That wasn't any animal, Frank. That thing was a beast."

"All animals can be beasts, Kiri."

Frank began to walk away, *what a fucking waste of lives*, stepping over the rubble towards the exit. He heard Kiri shout out to him.

"Aren't you going to help these people, Frank?!"

"Help them? They're all dead, Kiri. But there's a little girl out I may still be able to help, that is provided I haven't wasted enough time already."

Kiri, determined to keep him among the dead, continued to percolate apathy – the sweet sound of repudiation bubbling away. Much to her dismay, Frank carried on walking. She shouted - she had to really reach the back rows with her next lines:

"But why, Frankie? All this death surrounds us every day. People come and go; it's the way life is. Look at how still these people are now. They lay on the floor in perfect slumber, feeling neither comfort nor pain. Their bodies exist here, but we know they are long gone, don't we, Frank? Where do you think it is that they have gone? Perhaps it's somewhere beautiful, somewhere as peaceful as their limp corpses."

Frank looked back at all the bodies who were littered around Kiri as she began to heave her cart back onto its feet. The poor souls: some had broken backs; others had crushed heads. But Frank understood what Kiri meant by their peacefulness. There was something in the utter stillness of these figures that he envied. Frank thought the way the bodies no longer reacted to the weight of the gold columns forcing them into the floor was somewhat desirable, yet simultaneously *oddly pathetic*. He began to wonder at all why he did have an urge to search out this missing girl. She had been missing since morning. Would she still need Frank's help? Surely her father would have found her by now, or if not her father, somebody else... perhaps something unspeakable had happened to her? He tried not to think about that possibility, but Frank knew the world contained such evil, he was often reminded of it in reverberations of darkness from strangers he met in his occupation: Pickpockets, shoplifters, dealers, junkies, weirdos, perverts, peeping-toms... *diddlers*. What a cruel joke it could all be. Kiri – who had managed to get the cart fully upright now- shouted across one last time.

"You alright, Frankie? You look about ready to weep... Oh, don't shy away from me, Frank. It's alright, really." He dragged his feet back to the cart, he was *welling up, and lost*. There was no need for Kiri to shout anymore. In fact, she practically whispered.

"And there was me thinking you hadn't a care for these people, you almost had me going there... Come here sweetheart, there, there... I've got an idea, why don't I make us both a nice black coffee to keep us going, eh? We can sit with these folks while we drink it. We could stay as long as we want, Frank. Nothing can stop us staying with them; perhaps we'll stay here long enough to become like them. Doesn't that sound tranquil, Frankie? Well, I'm going to have to break the tranquillity for just a second, though. I need to grind the beans Frank, cover your ears if you must... Anyway, here we go... YEP, THIS WHOLE PLACE IS GOING TO FALL APART NOW, IT'S ONLY A MATTER OF TIME. The Birdcage was the only thing which kept it stable. Everyone knows that, from central management and the landlord all the way down to little old me... Why don't we just stay right here and watch it fall around us, eh?" Kiri nestled up against Frank's shoulder. He could feel the heat from her body soothe him. This scenario had played out many times inside Frank's imagination in the past. He clasped his arm around her shoulder and took a deep breath in. She smelled sweet, akin to cinnamon and vanilla. Kiri moved a hot coffee mug into his hand to move him into a further level of comfort and warmth.

"I knew you'd fall for me, Frank... Everyone does." She firmly grabbed Frank's hand and pushed the hot cup to his lips. Frank took a sip.

"Doesn't that make you feel warm and safe, Frank? Drink the whole thing, now... You can join our friends here soon enough."

Frank looked around at all the bodies and he took another swig of the coffee. It tasted fresh and rich. As it slid down his throat, he could feel the warmth move down. When it reached his chest, it felt somewhat hotter. It left a burning sensation in his heart. So much so in fact that he hunched over from the pain. By the time the black liquid reached his stomach, the heat was unbearable. He could feel it searing the walls of his stomach and causing acid to rise and rise, bubbling up from his *fuzzy belly*, up to his *greedy gullet*.

"One more sip, Frankie... Almost there."

Kiri pushed the cup towards his lips once more. But before Kiri could tip the container into Frank's mouth, a hand stopped it. Frank recognised the way the hand contorted itself elegantly to reach the top of the cup. The hand used only it's pinkie and ring finger to push the cup down to the floor. Frank had only ever known his wife to use such an odd combination of digits to move things - he found it so peculiar and endearing that he mentioned it to Sarah every time she did it. This was undeniably Sarahs technique, Frank thought. But it didn't take long for him to feel the rim of the cup pressing against his own ring and pinkie as he pushed it down. It was his hand, and his choice, but he knew deep down that Sarah's influence was the driving force. The handle of the cup snapped off as it hit the tiles on the floor.

Frank awaited Sarah's voice to comment on the mess it made, but no such comment came. Kiri peeled away from Frank as he stared right through her in pure silence. She cowered, as it was only in this moment that she realised how imposing he could be. Frank could feel Sarah with him, and the burning sensation subsided. He rose to his feet and took a deep breath.

"I think that's the last of your drinks I'll ever have, Kiri."

Frank followed the trail of paw marks, scratched shop windows, and still-settling dust towards the exit of the mall. As he reached the *end of the line*, adjacent to the exit doors, and basked in the light which broke in through the glass double doors, his trail ended. It led up to the entrance of the last standing shop in the mall: Thomas Young's Instruments and Accessories.

13

The aftermath of the chaos caused by Artemis chasing the girl was stark; the mall was not much more than a maze of broken glass, dirty foot and paw prints, and knocked over litter bins. Soiled Styrofoam fast food containers, discarded newspapers, and *shredded* toy packaging was mosaicking the floor, *like rotting leaves in the garden - needs raking up.* As he waded through the garden refuse towards Thomas Young's Instruments and Accessories, Frank noticed an increasing amount of shattered glass peeking out through the rest of the rubbish, *Buckshot Road after New Year's.* One might have assumed, by glancing at the music store's exterior, that it was hit worst of all by the unseasonable Hogmanay. However, Frank recognised that the appalling condition of the shop was consistent with how its appearance had been for the last ten years. Cracked windows, half a sign, and even missing bricks in the wall – *Leave those kids alone!* Frank saw the trail of coffee-stained paw prints *Nick Masoning* up to the store front and *slipping into ghost notes* underneath the gap created by the door - which hung crooked on a single hinge, swinging *out of time.* Thomas Young, Instruments and Accessories had once been a shining gem embedded within the mall. It was the first shop to open all those years ago when the ribbon cutting ceremony declared the mall open. Back then, jazz was the popular style of music and Thomas Young's shop boasted the widest range of 'horns' - cornets through to tubas. Brass, woodwind, double bass, percussion, keys, it even had a selection of classical guitars imported from Spain. When Frank was a boy, he couldn't stand jazz, *bunch of beret-topped bonces clicking their fingers to the wrong notes*. When his father used to play jazz records in the family home, Frank could be heard calling it messy. *Mum spent all day cleaning the house then you come back and make it sound untidy*. Little Franklin couldn't understand why people liked it. He couldn't even think while it was on, *can't do my after-school sums with double-time swing spinnin' my brain out*, let alone read the paper like his father did. It was only once Frank grew into an adult that he finally grew a taste for it, much like a growing boy does for his dad's beer, or tobacco. Once his palette had grown accustomed to clarinets and ride cymbals, he was destined to annoy Sarah with a *polycanorous* record collection of his own.

"Frank, do you really have to play such busy music?" Sarah found it more busy rather than messy, but the *schoolboy* sentiment remained. Frank could get caught up in the 'busy' noise. He'd often daydream about playing in the band, he always thought he'd make a good bass player due to his large palms and *heavy sausage fingers*. He'd go into a trance miming along to the tracks. He'd leave his body in the armchair by the record player while his mind and heart were on stage in a smoky bar - which was typically dimly lit with red cloth covered circular tables. Usually, the trance would push him into dozing off; and often, Sarah would

171

wake him at the end of the record's side by applauding her husband's 'performance'. He'd sharply wake and the two of them would giggle like mischievous children about the whole thing.

"I was in a quintet this time."
Frank would tell Sarah so she could share in his little fantasy.

"Oh, I know, Frank, and you played wonderfully darling. Snoring away through your big bassoon!"
More than the romance, more than the support, more than the beautifully cooked *double-helping* meals on the weekends, Frank missed the shared jokes, the laughter. This sentimentality washed over Frank like a wave, then drained away at his feet as he heard the malevolent and discordant laughter of young lads abusing the instruments, *how is it they're making everything sound like a bleeding bagpipe?* He could hear strings breaking, drums splitting, and wooden necks snapping before they all came spilling out from the entrance – completely *doing in* the door on their way.

"Oi! You little terrors, get out of here!"
The boys dropped whatever item each of them was *mucking about with* and fled out the shop, through the adjacent exit, and into the rain-glazed streets. All but one, who fell to the floor and propped themselves against the shop windowsill, amongst all the rubble and shards he hung his head.

"What are you still doing here?" Frank said as he marched towards the boy. "You shouldn't be causing trouble for the shop owners like that, let alone this place isn't safe for the public anymore, you need to leave. Now!"
As Frank drew closer, he could see the boy was in *about as much of a state as the horn shop*. The boy had bruises all

about his face, arms, and legs. Presumably, his torso was just as *peppered* with bright green and purple *seasoning*. Frank could not however, confirm the existence, nor the severity of those marks as the boys' frayed, torn, and soiled home-made jumper obscured them. Frank knelt down to the boy, *meet their level*, who was staring into the near distance, *one who's distracted with melancholy often does, I know I do*. As he got closer, Frank could smell the unmistakable odour of stale urine, *the lavvy in The Turncoats*, he did his best to contain his reactions to the acrid waft but his expression still showed a little.

"Are you lost, lad?"

The boy did not move, and his eyes continued to look outward, as if Frank was just a spectre whispering in his ear.

"Do you need me to call your mother?"

The boy pulled his knees towards his chest and buried his head in his arms.

"Perhaps your father?"

The boy sharply turned his head away from Frank. He had clearly struck a nerve. Frank attempted to communicate with the boy on a different subject.

"Why didn't you run off like all've your friends?"

The boy squirmed a little, then - with his head buried back in his arms, and muffled through his chunky-knit sleeves - finally spoke.

"They're not my friends."

Frank looked towards the door which the other two boys had ran out through and followed their dirty footprints back to the child who was trying to mitigate the sound of his crying, *sniffing and whining*. Frank paused for a moment before trying to open a dialogue with the child again.

"Well, they're gone now. It's just you and me. My name's Frank."

Frank extended his hand to the boy, who flinched at the very movement.

"You're going to arrest me. Aren't you, sir?"

Frank, puzzled, retracted his hand.

"Arrest you? For what, getting punched in the face? Whatever makes you think I would arrest you?"

"You're the second police officer I've been caught by today. I'm sure I'm not lucky enough to be let off the hook twice in the same day. It's the other boys' fault, they make me misbehave for their own amusement. If I don't do it, they beat me, sir. I told the other policeman that I wouldn't do it again, that I would rather let them beat me to death before I misbehave for them again... But the pain, they punched, kicked, one even nutted me in the forehead, see it? It hurt so much I couldn't take it anymore. I was scared, sir, scared of dying. I told the other policeman that I wouldn't be, but I couldn't help it! Mostly, I was scared of how it would upset my mother. I couldn't help it, sir. I suppose that makes me a coward as well as a criminal... Well, if you must lock me up then so be it, at least I couldn't cause any more harm if I was put behind bars."

The boy's *schnoz* was *dripping uncontrollably* as he extended both of his arms and offered his wrists to be handcuffed. Frank, attempting to relax the young lad with a calm chuckle, gently pushed the boy's hands back.

"What on earth makes you think I'm a police officer?"

"Your clothes, of course. You're wearing the same uniform as the police officer I got caught by this morning."

"I'm... I'm a security guard, lad." Frank said, slightly confused, "That's all... not a policeman, just a lowly, powerless, security guard."

The boy wiped his nose with the sleeve of his jumper, *Might as well, it's already soiled*, then rubbed his eyes dry with his knuckles. He looked up at Frank and analysed the security guard's attire, muttering to himself all the while.

"But, the other man, he-"

"Never mind all that. What's your name, son?"

"Salian... My name is Salian, sir."

"Well, Salian, as mentioned before, my name is Frank. I'm the head security guard here at the mall. My job is to help people should they need it, I have been hired to be of use to people within the mall, that is all. I can tell you're distressed, lad, and I only approached you to see if you needed some assistance. I am not in the business of punishing young boys who have already clearly been punished enough. By their peers, no less. Even if I did want to arrest you, I do not have the authority to arrest anyone. There is no reason to be intimidated or frightened, young man, I am here to serve you and to keep you safe. As you can plainly see, the mall is not in a safe condition to remain in at the moment. Now, would you like me to call your mother and have her pick you up? You'll have to wait outside for her to arrive."

"Please, no!" Salian desperately begged "My mother cannot come! Besides, she is still at work. And I couldn't wait outside! The other boys won't have gone far. They will be waiting for me nearby and they'll start on me again if I wait outside! Please don't make me stay outside, sir, please! Can't I stay in here with you? You look big and strong; the other boys wouldn't dare come near me if they saw you guarding me. Please let me stay in here. Please!"

Frank felt the desperation from Salian. He was pale and sickly; he was clearly tired of his harassers and exhausted from his experience of the world, *his world at least*, he clung onto Frank's jacket sleeve and pressed his forehead into Frank's shoulder as he pleaded. Frank lightly shook his head.

"Salian. One can't hide from dangers all the time. Dangers will always be waiting for you. There are dangers outside as you have said, but there are also dangers in here. This place is slowly collapsing, there won't be any safety here soon enough, do you understand?"

Salian regretfully nodded his head and told Frank that he understood. Frank saw how tormented this boy was. *No child should have to experience this amount of cruelty this young*. Frank could see that Salian had experienced the darker corners of the world, and set in this child's face, were the lethargic eyes of an adult. Frank sighed and then continued his train of thoughts out loud.

"However, I think you have faced plenty of these dangers for one day. Don't you?"

As Salian nodded, some of the defeat in his eyes waned, and some colour – *other than green and purple* – waxed on his cheeks.

"Yes... Well, young man, I think you have indeed deserved a respite. I have but one more errand to run here in the mall before I can leave though. Would you like to accompany me?"

"Yes please, sir! Anything! I'll do the errand for you if you'll let me stay with you for a while! Even if it's cleaning the toilets!"

Frank chuckled at the young boy's eagerness, *be careful what you wish for*, but as Salian leapt to his feet, Frank was also rudely reminded of the urine smell coming from Salian's tatty jumper.

"Very well, Salian." Frank turned his head away from the *pissy pullover.* "However, if you are to accompany me you shall be doing so as part of my security team, understood? Good. And as part of my security team, you must adhere to certain standards. I run a tip-top group of security guards here at the mall, a very tight ship indeed, and much like the military, I expect my officers to be wearing the proper uniform."

Frank raised his eyebrows and nodded towards Salian's torn, soiled jumper.

"That garment simply will not do, Security Officer Salian. Before we can proceed with any of our duties you must remove it and present yourself as a security officer." Frank – holding his breath, *no worse than picking up after Artemis* - helped Salian remove the sodden jumper and placed it into the nearest bin. Salian looked very upset about this, as if he had lost something of sentimental value. But his frown was soon remedied as Frank removed his own blazer and placed it over the boy's shoulders. Salian's eyes grew wider than ever before as he let his arms be swallowed by the sleeves of the engulfing jacket, *krill in a baleen.* Salian admired the stitching and the officiality of the garment that was frankly more of a cloak than a jacket for the young man. The two *growing boys* smiled at each other, it soothed them equally. Salian was so glad someone was finally helping him and Frank appreciated being appreciated, *maybe I'm not such a useless old fool after all*. Frank crouched down and turned away from Salian, he nodded at his newest recruit over his shoulder.

"Hop on then."

Salian eagerly jumped onto Frank's back, both of them wobbled slightly as Frank got himself upright. Frank could feel Salian's little feet digging into the tops of his thighs as he tried to maintain his balance. Salian jostled his little forearms a little too tightly around Frank's shoulders and neck, *the sleeper hold!* And his bony torso dug into Frank's spine. But, even with all of this discomfort taken into consideration, Frank proudly carried Salian, *riding in on a donkey*, and the pair entered the music shop.

14

To avoid receiving *yet another bludgeoning,* Frank had to duck under the timber lintel - which was hanging on by a nail *and a wish,* the others of which were protruding from the *crusty, warped frame* - Frank stooped to *allow the boy safe passage,* and Salian covered his head with his blazer-protected elbows. It was clear that Thomas Young, Instruments and Accessories had been glorious in its heyday, but now all but one lightbulb had popped - and never been replaced. Dust-plated and cobweb-cloaked orchestral instruments of every variety were mounted up and down the double-storied walls, or, at least the ones where the mounts hadn't fallen out after *buggering up the plaster.* Even the brick face of the mezzanine stairs looked like a *bloody general's jacket,* the way the medals of capos, tuners, resin blocks, reeds, and packs of strings decorated it, all the way up to its snapped wooden hand rails. Frank could hear the sound of rustling papers and pensive muttering coming from the elevated platform, and a thick plume of pale blue smoke curled like fiddleheads as it gently rolled down each step. The cloud reached the pair and the smell of toasted tobacco made Salian cover his mouth and sputter

179

into his sleeve as his eyes watered. Frank took a deep, familiar breath in.

"Hello?"

Frank called up. He hoped for more of a response than the inaudible grumbling he received from *the rude old git*. He looked over his shoulder to address Salian.

"Is that the shop owner up there?"

"I think so. The other boys call him 'the man in the box'. He never comes down from there and it always sounds like he's very preoccupied with his papers."

Frank called up to the man in the box a second time and received a similar grumbling to the first, only slightly louder this time. Frank thought he made out the last part of what the man said; something along the lines of '*well, then come up here*'.

The weight of Salian on Frank's back slowed him down a little, as keeping his balance became a struggle while lifting his feet over the debris of fallen instruments, knocked over bookshelves, and loose papers which littered the floor. He thought of asking Salian to get down but – *couldn't do that, funny little lad'd step on something sharp, I can feel glass crunching under me shoes. Or he'll slip on the papers and knock his head or something. Best keep hold of him for now. Feels like my shoulder's gonna give way any minute though.* Frank kept quiet as he traversed the clutter, other than the occasional grunt - *turning into a rude old git m'self.* The poor lighting made this task even more difficult, and when Frank had the idea to hold onto the wall for more stability, *bannister'd give me splinters*, the bricks crumbled at his touch and clattered onto the floor. The noise reverberated around the room and Frank heard the man in the box viciously whisper, *like a cartoon snake.*

"Oh, for heavens' sake be quiet! You'll wake him up! It's a fairly simple path, just follow the ashtrays, they'll lead you up here."

Frank squinted at the floor and could see a trail of dirty ashtrays – *explains the crunching* - filled to the brim with cigarette butts and sooty residue. He followed them as instructed and it did seem to be a slightly more stable route, there was even some decent room to place his feet. He pushed a fallen ladder to one side as quietly as he could, *who's sleeping up there anyway?* And began to climb the curved staircase which led up to the 'box'.

"Excuse me, sir. My name is Frank Mossan, I'm the head of security here. I just wanted to ask you a few questions abou-"

"Shh!"

A figure rushed up to meet Frank and Salian at the top of the stairs. He was a svelte man, presumably in his fifties. He sported very worn dress shoes, torn black denim trousers, and a striped oxford shirt which may have –at one point in its life – had a collar attached to it – *pocket's been torn an'all.* The man had wild, unkempt locks of dark grey hair that was held tightly to the sides of his parietal by an old elastic band. His hair - what was left of it - joined up at the temples with his facial hair which hadn't seen a razor in a very long time. The man pressed a very yellowed finger up to Frank's mouth to hush him. Frank, in his discomfort in the physicality of this gesture, *let alone how musty it is* - and the many possibilities swimming around his mind as to what the yellow stains on this man's finger could be from - began to awkwardly scan the room. He noticed that up on the mezzanine, everything - including violin f holes - had been used as an ashtray, and Frank was then oddly comforted by the recognisable scent of stale tobacco coming from the man's finger. In a very hushed tone, the man began to reprimand Frank.

"What do you think you're playing at? Coming in here, making all that noise, unbelievable! And then you just decided to waltz your way up here before I told you it was alright to do so?!"

"I do apologi-" The man glared at Frank and Frank immediately lowered his voice. "Apologies, sir. But I thought you said to come up here when I called you a minute ago."

"I did no such thing!"

"I thought I heard you say 'well then come up here'?"

"No, no, no. You misheard me. Perhaps you need your ears cleaning out you stupid fool. I didn't say 'well then come up here' I said 'watch the cat up here'. You two very well nearly woke him up too!"

Frank gave out a little sigh, the conversation was *more difficult than carrying Salian's dense little soul up the stairs*.

"I'm sorry if I disturbed your cat."

"It's not *my* cat. It just ran in here growling and roaring. It sprinted past my desk and went to sleep right over there."

The man pointed with his *pale carrot* towards a large pile of furniture, papers, and instruments in the darkest corner of the mezzanine. Slowly swishing back and forth at the base of this heap was a very large orange and black striped tail.

"You could have got us all bloody killed coming in here like that."

The man stopped himself long enough to take his wireframe glasses which were *hanging on for dear life* from his shirt pocket and gave them a wipe with his dirty shirt sleeve before resting them on his oily nose. He squinted through the smeared lenses at the boy on Frank's back.

"You've got some nerve coming back in here, lad. Where are your little friends this time, eh? Off ruining some other working stiff's business?"

Salian, hiding most of his face behind Frank's right shoulder, muttered back.

"They're not my friends."

The man adjusted his glasses again as they were not sitting on his nose the way he expected them to – *too slippery for 'em*. He noticed the bruising around Salian's face, and lessened his accusatory tone, while still saving face.

"Well, I should think not. The way they've left your face looking. Bloody great shiner that one on your eye'll turn out to be."

Frank could feel Salian tense up from the inspection he was receiving from the shopkeeper. Frank caught the shopkeeper's eye and flashed him a warning. The man stammered and tripped over his words for a second before continuing.

"I-I mean it looks quite painful. You must be a pretty tough young fellow, eh? My name is Mr. Holliday, by the way. I've got some ice by my desk; it'll reduce the swelling. Would you like to come and sit down?"

Frank and Salian looked at each other, then back to Mr. Holliday, and nodded in unison. The trio shuffled over and sat at the desk. Mr. Holliday began to parse through all the litter and rubble which populated the entirety of his workspace - including the drawers - to look for some ice for the boy's eye. Mr. Holliday was pulling out knick-knacks, papers, trinkets, broken pieces of stock, smoking paraphernalia, and general bric-a-brac, muttering to himself

183

all the while. Imagining that this search could go on for a *country minute*, Frank took another attempt at having a smooth conversation with the man.

"As I was saying, Mr. Holliday, my name is Frank Mossan, I'm the head of security here. I just wanted to ask you a few questions about a missing child. I watched her on the security cameras get chased past your shop. Salian, would you be so kind as to check the pocket of my blazer you're wearing? There should be a photograph in there." Salian rummaged for a couple of seconds then fruitfully produced the requested article with a proud smile on his face.

"Thank you, Salian... This is the picture I have of her, sir. However, she did appear older in the video footage so please bear in mind she may not have appeared exactly as you see in this photograph. Do you recognise her at all?" Frank shifted some of the *useless shit* aside and placed the photograph in front of Mr. Holliday who once again, smeared his glasses before examining it.

"Oh, I should say so," He chuckled. "Couldn't get a more up to date photo than this, eh? Still, I do recognise her. She was much older than this though, almost a woman, really. But I'd recognise her anywhere. Yes, she came in not long before you did. She was being chased by that bloody cat over there. It probably would've got her too if it didn't get distracted by your 'colleague' and his 'friends' who were mucking about vandalising my shop. As soon as it could smell them it beelined right in here. That girl managed to usher them all out before they became the next flavour of Whiskas and threw something – a toy I think – up here to distract it. It's been over there guarding it ever since."

"I see... And where were you, Mr. Holliday, when this was all occurring?"

"Same place as I am now." He slapped the frayed leather arms of his desk chair and gave a half-smile back to Frank. "I don't often leave this spot. You can observe the whole shop from up here."

"But you didn't think to intervene?" Frank asked "You didn't feel the need to helps the young boys? The lady in question? You didn't even have the impulse to move away once the tig-err-cat ran up here?"
Mr. Holliday let out a big sigh.

"For what?" He replied. "Should I have helped the group of kids who were wrecking my shop? Should I have helped the girl who was enough of an adult to act autonomously? Should I have attempted to take down the animal which is only acting as animals do, on its instincts?"

"Surely any of those options would have been better than to do nothing." Frank replied.
Mr. Holliday looked Frank up and down with a smirk.

"Would they have, Mr. Mossan? Tell me, how long have you worked in this mall?"
Frank looked around and puffed his cheeks while he tried to recall the years.

"A long old time Mr. Holliday. Decades in fact."

"Decades, you say? Well, I've had my shop here since before you were born, and possibly it will still stand long after you're gone. Yet, this is the first time we've ever met, isn't that right?"
Mr. Holliday began to deftly roll a cigarette – *one-handed, must've done time* – as he continued his *inaugural address*.

"You'd have thought with all those years our paths would have crossed once or twice - so why not? I'll admit a younger me, perhaps a naiver me, would have thought it a good idea to go rushing to the aid of children or girls being chased by animals. However, the years have passed, and over those years many complaints, reports, and pleas have been filed by me to the central management and even, in desperate times, to the landlord about the crimes and dangers that go on down here." He paused again briefly to wet the gum of his cigarette paper. "Not once did I receive a reply. Why should they? I was paying rent for my storefront to central management, and I was maintaining the premises as agreed in the contract for the landlord. What incentive do they have to address my problems? Neither care for the little people, and both are indistinguishable and interchangeable." As Mr. Holiday struck a match and lit his vice, starting it up with small, sharp, rhythmic puffs; Frank thought it was an opportune time to bring the conversation back to something with more utility.

"Did you see which way the girl went after getting the boys away?"
Mr. Holliday looked a Frank from over the rim of his glasses for a moment while pushing smoke out from his nostrils, followed by a precursory sigh.

"So, I decided to stop keeping up my end of the agreement you see. No more monthly rent being posted off to central management, and no more laborious maintenance to keep in good faith with the landlord. I simply stopped. And, do you know, it's been years!" Mr. Holliday chuckled, "Can you imagine! Although I must admit, at first, I was a little upset that the absence of my duties went unnoticed by both of the powers-that-be, but after a while I found it was in fact extremely liberating. When a year or so passed, I concluded that the central management were so swamped with inefficiency and incompetence that they would never notice I had not been paying my rent. Once this revelation hit me, I realised I no longer had any need to make any money from my business - as the rent is where the majority of my sales were going. It was just as well really, as due to my wilful and liberating neglect of my responsibility to maintain the shop, I hadn't seen a customer for at least six months. Shoplifters and other ne'er-do-wells started coming in as word got around the underbelly of society that I would not intervene in their various dealings. 'There's a bloke who owns a music shop, he don't even care if you pinch aught, he just smiles and waves.' And it's true, sometimes I do wave at them as they scuttle off with enough music manuscripts to score a fix. The truth is I have no incentive to act contributory anymore."

By this point Frank had attempted to get a word in a few times throughout Mr. Holliday's one-man production - to no avail. Salian could see Frank was becoming weary of the tirade of speech coming from his agitator. He kept alternating his gaze between the two adults and saw subtle similarities in speech patterns, body language, and even physicality. Mr. Holliday had verbally captured Mr. Mossan. Not because Mr. Mossan was a weak man, Salian thought, but rather because Mr. Holliday was using the invisible tethers of civility to restrain him, by proxy Mr. Holliday held the both of them verbally hostage. The longer Salian observed, the easier it became for him to see the faces of all his bullies projected onto the shopkeeper's head. Salian, very aware that he was wearing the jacket of a senior security guard, was getting ready to transform himself from a child into a useful colleague and member of the security team. All the shopkeeper's talk of laziness was starting to annoy Salian. He could feel his face grow increasingly warm, and his body was becoming very itchy as Mr. Holliday continued.

"So that's how you see the shop in the state it is in now. I'll be the first to admit that its appearance is undesirable. But the freedom and time I have gained to pursue my interests now that I've shirked my duties is phenomenal. I read all day, I nap whenever I want, should I ever get hungry I imagine there's some food laying around here somewhere. I've even taken up origami; I'm progressing rather quickly if I do say so myself. Would you like to see some? I keep them in my drawer down here... Here we are, this one is a crane – a classic shape really. Once I got comfortable with the folds, I began to experiment with shapes of musical instruments. Here is a viola, this one is a cello, I made a guitar – here it is, then there's a double-bass, and another vio-"

"Enough! Which way did the girl go?! My colleague needs to know he's on a very important mission!" Salian had finally cracked. He slammed his fists on the table as he shouted this order which rang through the whole shop. Mr. Holliday's face was frozen stiff, Salian's outburst had terrified him. *'That shut the old fool up'* thought Salian. As he looked over to Frank for some sort of affirmation, he noticed that Frank was displaying a similar petrified expression. Frank grabbed Salian and jolted both of them from the desk as a loud roar rang out and a spatter of blood flecked across Salian's face. Before young Salian could comprehend what had happened, what was left of Mr. Holliday was scattered in a few bloody chunks on the floor. A flash of orange and black hurtled towards Salian, but not before he was knocked to the floor by Frank who had intercepted the mauling. Frank was now on the floor wrestling amongst the *offal* which had constituted Mr. Holliday mere seconds ago. He had managed to lock the beast's paws in his grips, but it was still bearing down on top of him, snapping its jaws at his face.

"Salian! Run! I'm not going to hold it for long! Get away quickly! Get to your mother!"
Within those few seconds, Salian experienced a lifetime of decision making. The world felt as if it slowed down for the first time since Salian had begun wishing for such a miracle years ago, *just like Captain Time from my comics.* He imagined himself running down the stairs. He conjured images of Frank succumbing to the claws and fangs which inevitably found their way into his body. He thought of how his mother would weep for her boy being in such danger – *how could I let this happen to you? She'll say* - how she would likely quit her job to make sure her defenceless son was never alone and in harm's way again. He thought of how he would weep himself, for letting Frank die only to mourn him pitifully afterwards. He saw a coward's future, running from beating after beating, shying from confrontation, and having the world walk over him for an eternity. *What are you gonna do about it, Salian? What're you gonna do?* Then, as all these scenarios flashed in front of Salian, something odd happened. He took in a deep, slow breath and – like he was possessed by a spirit of primal focus, *just like The Red Ninja!* – he grabbed a pen from Mr. Holliday's desk, and calmly pushed it through the animal's eye. It felt like it was being pushed through wet sand as it entered the centre of the thing's skull. Then he felt the whole weight of the animal shift into the pen as it dropped to the floor. Salian stood frozen still; he couldn't even blink. He watched Frank roll

the mass of fur and teeth to one side as he got to his feet. He could hear Frank ask him some questions as he knelt next to him, but Salian could make none of the words out. Everything seemed muffled and far away. His body felt separate from himself, like he was a stranger pulling levers inside a Salian-shaped mechanism, *Man-Bot*. He stood there for a moment while Frank stood near him with one of his big, dry hands on his shoulder in a poor attempt at comforting the boy. After a short while, Salian no longer felt so far away. He still felt like a stranger, but now he was a stranger who could do a convincing Salian impression.

"I'm ok."

He said, monotonously, his gaze firmly on the four-legged carcass in front of him.

"No." Said Frank, "You're not. Not yet... But you will be, lad... Thanks, mate."

Both of them remained staring at the dead animal. Frank noticed that inside the eye socket which Salian had perforated, there were no viscous remains one would expect from such a wound. The pen rattled around in the empty eye socket with no signs of physical trauma. The rest of the head was also clear of injuries and blood. Its fangs were almost too-white as they protruded from its short snout. Its ears tapered into too-perfect of an arc at the tips. The orange and black fur was beautiful, and was delicately accented by one glinting amber eye which seemed to follow Frank as he moved to the other side of its body.

"Uncanny."

He saw much of the same fur running over its angular shoulders, huge paws, and elongated tail. All but one part of its body. Its foreleg still had the same mottled grey pattern as Frank remembered. Although Frank was *of course* glad to

190

see Salian still alive. And, although Frank knew that that beast would have soon transformed past the point of no return into an abomination. Part of it was still Artemis, *my good girl, my little taxi*. He felt the guilt of his neglect overcome him, and he did his best not to weep. He began blinking uncontrollably and, to retain some semblance of discipline – *for the boy's sake* - Frank tried looking at something further away than the desk, or the remains of Mr. Holliday, or the animal carcass. He looked at the walls of the shop, he noted all of the instruments on them. Frank thought about music, how each of the pieces had the potential to be part of beautiful compositions, perhaps in the clumsy hands of a student still *getting his chops*, or even in the nimble fingers of a master, capable of expressing the most emotive of melodies. It wasn't long after this that Frank realised how wasted that potential could be, *how long have they been gathering dust on these walls?* He felt compelled to take one with him. It was not the correct thing to do, but it *felt right* at that moment. He timidly walked up to the nearest wall and a violin caught his eye. Its shape, its elegance, its sonic beauty, much like a siren it cried out to him to be saved. Frank extended his arm out to it and ran his forefinger across the slick, lacquered, spruce wood grain. His eyes lit up like that of a child's, then they illuminated with a cold realisation. Upon removing his fingers from the instrument, he had noticed he had left a scar on it. The scar started bubbling and quickly peeled the varnish clean off the wood. Following suit, the wood began to rot quickly before his very eyes. The tension of the still-tuned strings was of course too much for the dying wood to bear, and it inevitably gave way under the pressure. The neck of the violin *slingshotted* across the room and the wood of its body shattered magnificently. The timbre shrapnel flew across the room, missing both Frank and Salian, but hitting every instrument in the shop. A chain reaction occurred, wood rotted, brass melted, ivory turned to dust, and the cacophony of wailing and wheezing quickly turned into a deathly silence. Frank's eyes stung and he apologised to Salian as he blamed the conveniently unsettled dust in the shop for his tears.

"It's ok, Frank... I cry all the time."
Salian said, returning the hand-on-the-shoulder gesture just as awkwardly as he had seen Frank perform it. Frank wiped his eyes and nose on his shirt sleeve.

"Come on, lad. Let's get you to your mother, eh?"
Frank picked the boy up and placed him on his back once more, wincing as he did. Salian quickly repositioned his hand from Frank's shoulder as the shirt sleeve was wet through with blood.

"It's Mr. Holliday's."
Grunted Frank as he carried the young boy back down the rickety stairs. He was slower than he was on the way up. But oddly enough, Salian felt lighter on the old man's back than he did before. *Never a burden, kids.*

15

The stairs heaved, bowed, and groaned under Frank's shoes as he carried Salian back down to the shop floor. He saw how the gnarled cracks in the dark, dry wood were symptomatic of the half-exposed black iron nails that jutted out from the walls in all directions. There was *no way* they still held the structure together. As Frank tentatively waddled onto the final step, the thing gave way. *Bloody typical, last step an'all,* Frank thought as he and the boy crashed into the floor. On his way down, *arse over tit,* Frank saw he was heading into some *suspiciously jagged* detritus. Instinctively, Salian was launched away from the spot, *hopefully out of harm's way.* The old man landed on his back onto something *round and metal.* The wind was *completely knocked out* of his *sails,* and he stayed prone for a moment, mouthing words until his lungs could fill back up. Once Frank could puff his chest out again, he righted himself, dusted himself off – *fag ash on me trousers* - and tried to spot Salian, but he was nowhere to be seen.

"Salian!"

Frank cried out with what little breath was still in his *sails.*

"Frank! I'm over here!"

Frank looked over a vast ocean of desks and instruments, filing cabinets and ashtrays, receipt slips and printed symphonies, and out *well past the buoys* he saw a small hand raised up like a periscope, thrashing around in the *Bent Tuba Triangle*.

"Salian, stay there, I'm coming over."
Frank ordered as he began to wade into the clanking tide, hopping up on the odd tabletop every now and then to get a good view of his safest path.

"Salian, where are you? Raise your hand again would you, lad."
The boy's hand appeared again, but further from Frank than it previously was.

"Stop moving, I'm coming to get you but you must stay still."

"I haven't moved Frank, I swear! Please come and get me Frank, I can't see anything in all this mess! Some of it is giving me splinters and I can hear glass crunching under my feet!"
Oh, for goodness' sake.

"If you can hear glass crunching then you must be moving your feet, Salian. Please, stop moving."

"I promise, Frank, I'm not moving! I can feel the glass swimming around my ankles, and something keeps pushing me! It's scratchy, Frank! Please hurry!"
As Frank waded up to his armpits in the heap of retail furniture and musical instruments, he came across a mahogany bureau to clamber on top of. It was unstable, *feels like it's not touching the floor.* His feet manically see-sawed as he slowly stood upright on top of the teetering narrow peak of the bureau - its locked hatch applauded him all the while. Frank looked for Salian once more. He saw a

silhouette standing in the exit of the shop, but it was not the silhouette of a young boy; the frame was that of a young woman. The figure appeared to be carrying something in her hands as the arms of the outline stopped at the elbows and, presumably, continued out in front of her. The image was facing Frank with purpose; he could feel her gaze *scratching at me skin*. She stood there for a while, and her head tilted as she examined Frank, *waiting for me to make a move?* Frank, confused by the figure's presence, simply observed the woman. Very slowly, her hands returned to her side, and her left hand was in fact holding a small object. Frank squinted at the object and noticed the faintest ripple in the air above it, some heat was escaping from the object. Cautiously, Frank called out to Salian once more.

"Salian."

Before Salian could reply, the figure standing in the store's exit also called out.

"Salian! Oh! My son, my son, where are you, my son? Follow my voice, darling, my little Salian, I have brought you some hot cocoa. Come and drink it quickly before it gets cold!"

"Mum?" Salian replied "Is that you?"

Some hurried rustling came from the direction of his voice, but it quickly stopped.

"Why aren't you at work?"

"It is me, my love. The boss let me finish early. He had to close the tower so he could go for a swim, so I ordered him a cab to the pool and I was done for the day. Come here now, darling, your cocoa is getting cold as we speak."

Even though the tone of the woman's voice was unfamiliar, Frank recognised the woman's speech patterns. On the surface of all the furniture, Frank could see a line of shifting junk begin to carve its way towards the woman.

"Salian! Stop! That is not your mother, you mustn't go to her! I know that voice. She works in the mall. It is NOT your mother!"

The line carried on at a steady pace and the wake of litter stretched out further behind it. Salian's 'mother' called over to Frank.

"How rude of you, Frankie. Of course I'm his mother! What sort of sick joke would it be to pose as such?! Come on now Salian, just a little farther to go... That's it, good boy"

Instinctively, Frank dove into the brass and mahogany scrap *like Steptoe McDuck* and frantically trudged through it. Furiously knocking things over left and right as he did, he managed to set course into Salian's wake. He began to run through the parting Salian had made and – as he could finally see the soot and ash covered floor - Frank started to catch up to him. Papers flew in his face, old guitar strings caught at his ankles and invaded the eyelets of his shoes, and dresser drawers flew open into his head, but Frank took it all in his stride. He would worry about the bruises later, *they're not going anytime soon anyway*, for now he had to reach Salian.

"Come now, my son. This is no place for you, bogged down amongst all this clutter and clatter, all this noise and notation. Come to me, come hold my hand, drink your cocoa I've so kindly prepared for you, and you will never have to hear this awful din again. I promise."

The figure's hand plunged into the mess, it eagerly anticipated Salian's meek clutch.

Salian, almost within reaching distance, held his hand out towards the porcelain skin of the woman's slender fingers.

As he went to grab her manicured hand, his own began to *take off*, and flew above it. He felt Frank's hands under each of his armpits as he was lifted above the furniture. As his eye line ascended above it all he could finally see the woman. *That's not my mum!* He gasped like he was coming up for air, and as the woman beckoned him again, it was then obvious to him that this was not his mother's voice. Frank placed the boy's legs onto his shoulders to allow him to have a clear view of the woman. Salian clutched Frank's flotation device of a head, some of his fingers spanned over Frank's eyes as he pushed his cheek onto Frank's scalp and whispered.

"Frank...That's not my mother."

With these words the woman screamed. The dark liquid in the cup she was still extending froze over instantly and the bone china cracked and popped into a dozen pieces, some flew into the shop's mess, other pieces of the powder-white shrapnel – including the handle – embedded themselves into Kiri's face. She barely flinched, and her eyes were still piercing Salian. Kiri clutched her heart with one hand, and tugged at her hair with the other. She shrieked as she ripped out tufts of her hair into matted black balls, only to see them pass through her now-translucent hands. She began to fade, as did her screams, until only the echo of it remained rattling around the bells of the few remaining brass instruments. Salian felt that this echo may never end. Frank, on the other hand, had become accustomed to this echo a very long time ago, *emotional tinnitus,* he called it. He carried Salian out of the shop exit and set him down. The pair caught their breath for a while. No words were exchanged, for they knew what the other was feeling. *A universal betrayal. Same as any other.*

After Frank stubbed the embers of his cigarette out onto the faux-marble flooring, both he and Salian rose to their feet and pushed open the chrome and glass door which *by some fucking miracle* looked perfectly new and burnished. The illusion was quickly broken as it creaked *like my old spine* as Salian pushed it open with both hands – letting it swing fully into the outer wall, *let 'em all know we're leaving, lad*. They were outside, and the sun would still be up for an hour or so. It was *boiling* outside and the rays pounded down onto the concrete of the plaza. Frank shied away from the brightness of it all, as the way the light refracted through his glasses and accentuated the smears and grime on the lenses which made it harder to view the world. It made his eyes *ache*. What's more, one of the lenses had a crack running right through it from the scuffle he had just had. As the two of them plodded along, Frank pulled the *knackered, and expensive, mind!* spectacles from his face and attempted to clean them on his bloody rag of a shirt – *rose-tinted might be a nice change* - when he felt Salian grab his hand.

"Wait."

The young man said, squeezing Frank's hand with an assertiveness that surprised his elder. Frank stopped immediately and squinted ahead to see what the matter was. He couldn't make it out, but he quickly noticed the sound of traffic, horns, sputtering engines, and scraping chassis.

"We have to wait for the lights to change."

Salian said, his voice squeaking as he tried his best to take charge of the situation.

"Yeah, you're right... Good lad."

Frank felt as though he should pat Salian on the back in encouragement. *Don't want to get too mushy. Anyway, might*

198

be too familiar. Maybe a pat on the head-no, no too condescending. A smile? Pah, a smile, as if that wouldn't go unnoticed. Frank settled for an awkward nod of the head and a muttered grunt, *stuffed it.* The lights changed and a beeping sounded which signalled the two to safely cross the road. As Salian clasped Frank's *dirty mitts* over the pelican crossing, a loud screeching noise cried out. A driver, positively strangling his steering wheel, shouted out of his window at the two as if it was still his right of way. *He hasn't noticed the lights've changed, twit.* Frank glared over at the man in the car, but could only make out a fractal version of the driver through his *buggered* lenses. The man was clearly preoccupied with himself, even the dog in the passenger seat seemed despondent over the man's outburst. A shadow was dancing around the backseat, mocking the owner and his silly dog.

"Impatient fool," Frank said, well in earshot of the car. "You'll get nowhere quicker screaming at the world like that."

The pair reached the other side of the road and Frank withdrew his hand to clean his glasses.

"Thank you Salian, I couldn't see a bloody thing back there."

"That's ok Frank. It's the least I could do... My mother's work is just down the high street a bit."

"Righto. Do you know how to get there?"

"Yeah."

Frank extended his palm to suggest that the boy could lead the way. Salian, upon noticing this signal, smiled a little, took a deep breath in, puffed out his chest, and tried his best to fill out Frank's blazer - which was drowning his frame. The high street was quaint, the antithesis of the mall. Its singlelaned cobblestone road cut a straight line through the red and brown bricked shops which were all flogging items of only the most pleasing aesthetics. The shop signs were all hand painted, and the shop owners welcomed in browsers with real smiles. Not the smile of a casino owner, *forked tongue an'all*, but a genuine kind of smile, the type often seen at a family reunion – *like they're at a wedding... Or funeral, really... depending on who's kicked it*. They walked along the cobbles for a while. Every now and then Frank would show the crumpled photograph to passers-by – *due diligence an'all that*, and asked them if they had seen the girl in the picture, most of whom - seeing his appearance as that of a man who had clearly been up all-night fighting, and assumedly drinking too - recoiled from the inquisitive tramp. Murmurs of 'What does that old nonce want with a little girl?' and 'Don't look at him, he'll only ask for money.' were spoken behind Frank as he shlepped through the town. Salian, luckily heard little of the public's remarks of his *saviour* as he regularly skipped ahead, only pulling back after he realised that he was too far from Frank. In turn, Frank – opportunistically – used the moments of Salian's skipping ahead to check his shoulder. It was still bleeding, *bloody smarts too*. It hadn't stopped since those inch-wide claws had ripped into him in the music shop. The sting of it was almost too much for him to conceal from Salian, some dirt from the animal was packed into the lacerations which only added a *grainy, grating feeling. Like someone's shoved sand in there*. There was no moment to get it all out however, because Salian, much like an excited puppy, kept turning around to check Frank was keeping up. He was trying. Eventually the conveyor belt of charming, angular roofs and timber framing paused to make way for a river.

The cobblestones however, had no time to pause and formed a bridge over the speedy, brownish-green water. Salian, knowing they were about halfway to his mother's place of work, saw this landmark as a reason to speed up. He began to excitedly jog over the river but soon heard Frank's distant voice.

"Salian! Hold on. Come back here for a moment."
His clumsy feet – hindered by his oversized shoes, *mum said I'd grow into these*, stopped side by side *attenn-hut!* and he pivoted around to see Frank, still at the start of the bridge, beckoning him back. He was sitting at a bench, with both of his arms clutching the side furthest from Salian's view. Salian scurried over and sat beside him.

"Why have we stopped? Are you hurt?"
Frank chuckled, he pulled his arms into view and produced two wafer cones, each one with a generous dollop of vanilla ice cream adorning them, and handed one to Salian. When Salian took the ice cream, Frank chuckled again.

"I didn't know your eyes could open that wide!"
He smiled, before swiftly explaining his mundane choice of ice cream.

"I didn't know what flavour you liked, they had strawberry, chocolate, mint... all sorts of flavours. But I thought I'd play it safe and go with vanilla. I remember when I was a little boy I hated strawberries, and chocolate ice cream always tasted fake to me."
Salian, with a mouthful of vanilla ice cream, swinging his legs happily off the edge of the bench replied.

"Vanilla's my favourite!"
"Mine too." Smiled Frank.
Salian looked around, wiping his cheeks with his sleeve. He had a guilty countenance, like a child soon to be scolded.

"Shouldn't we get going though?"

Frank explained to Salian that his mother would still be at work for a good two or three more hours and that ten minutes for the two of them to enjoy an ice cream wouldn't go amiss, *'specially given what we just went through*. They sat there, staring out to the river with its perfectly crooked banks made of light cocoa mud, slick and wet, and its beautifully earthy water for a while before Frank spoke again.

"You know... My wife - Sarah, her name was - she would've been proud of us right now. I can picture her sitting on this bench with us, watching the golden sunset bounce off the water. She always told me I should enjoy the present more, 'Be in the moment, you silly old fool!' she used to say." He turned to Salian. "She would've liked you, y'know. I think you would've reminded her of me in a way. Tell me, Salian, what do you think of this river? What do you see when you look at it?"

Salian looked hard pressed for a moment, then he hazarded a guess at the answer Frank was looking for.

"Water?"

Frank tried his best not to spit out his ice cream in laughter but this only led to the frozen ivory lump coming out of his nostrils. He covered it with his hand and both of them laughed childishly while Frank fought off an eager brain freeze. After a few snorts and tight eye-shutting it soon subsided.

"Well, yes. Water is correct. But there is more. The way its bends are carving into the earth. The rushes growing at its edges. The silt it's carrying, maybe there's a small island being formed at the mouth of this river. Do you see up there on that roof, Salian? There's a nest of pigeons, do you

see them? They probably fly down to bathe in this river.
Somewhere along this river the water may be processed for
us to drink. It's flowing out to the sea, dispersing amongst
the fish and sea life, joining the current and travelling for
miles, then eventually it will come back inland, only to tour
round, have more pigeons bathe in it, have more ice cream
eating idiots marvel at it, and it will do this over and over.
You can't think about that when you're rushing ahead down
the road, can you?"
Frank finished the last bite of his cone as he waited for
Salian's answer.

"So, we drink the water. Then we wee it back out into
the river."
He said with the most serious of faces.

"Well, yes... I suppose you're right again!"
Frank laughed once more as he raised himself from the
bench.

"Come on then, let's get going."
The two crossed the bridge and passed more Elizabethan
shop fronts. The black timber frames' angles became parallel
with the incline of the large hill.

"It's just at the top of this."
Salian pointed to the zenith of the hill ahead of them.

"Oh, of course, it is." Frank sighed, "Bear with me,
Salian. My legs aren't quite what they used to be."
Salian could see Frank was concerned about reaching the
top of the hill. He heard Frank's complaint about his legs, but
the way the old man clutched at his shoulders belied his
excuses. Although Salian considered full well that the legs of
the *old fool* could still play a factor. Frank already looked out
of breath just craning his neck up to see the top. The young
boy tried to incentivise Frank.

"It's got a lovely view at the top. My mother always complains about the walk up, but never the scenery. I bet you can see more of the river from up there. Maybe you can spot the little island it's making."

Frank stared at the lad for a while, then nodded his head toward the hill.

"Last one up's a rotten egg."

Salian shot ahead as most excited children would when presented with a very achievable challenge. Frank tried to keep up, but settled for just keeping Salian in his sights as he clambered up, huffing and wheezing. At the top of the hill Frank could see a short wall surrounding a structure, possibly cordoning off the property's staff parking area. Salian was already waiting at the entrance of the structure and he appeared to be talking to someone on the other side of the wall. *Who is that boy talking to?* Frank hypothesised that it was probably a security guard such as himself, but picked up his pace to reach Salian, *just in case*. As he reached the top, the hill levelled out. He could see the building emerge over the crest. A high-rise office block, taller than he imagined, could possibly be hidden all the way up there. Frank was baffled how he didn't see it at the bottom of the high street - but nevertheless, there it was. Fifteen stories of space; He saw the top first, Peaked arches, chrome frames nesting reflective panes of glass. So shiny one could only see the blueness of the sky between the crosses of the metal frames, Frank's head immediately imagined a plane or helicopter being fooled by the illusion and smashing into the glass monolith, *everyone thinks it, don't they?* As he thought about the shards raining down, he noticed that after about five stories, the building was composed of huge industrial concrete slabs, stacked end to end, only interspersed occasionally with tiny windows only big enough to just about get your head through, *like bloody archer's windows, balister... balistrar... ...arrow slits.* The fortressed midriff of the property was finally finished off on the ground floor with the same brickwork as on the high-street. Only, the bricks had each been painted one of the three primary colours, with no real pattern or intended design, it looked like somebody had stacked a greenhouse on top of a prison which, in turn was atop a pile of children's building blocks. Frank was finally at the top of the hill, and could see over the short wall into what he had previously assumed to be a car park. It was certainly an asphalted area, but in lieu of flashy company cars and SUVs with dog hair covered interiors, he saw climbing frames, swing sets, hopscotch, sand pits, and children... many children. All of whom were running and screaming in delight; it was recess, and Salian was talking to a little girl –no more than five years old – over the wall.

"Why don't you play with us anymore, Salian?"

"I go to big boy school now, Polly. I can't anymore, I'm busy doing grown-up things. And I've got a job too!"

"But nobody else wants to push me on the swings here, they all want to do the climbing frame even though I told them that's boring."

"Surely somebody will, Polly? No?"
Frank gently interjected.

"Oh, go on Salian. Of course, you can push her on the swings. I'll go talk to one of the teachers here and explain we're looking for your mother. What's her name?"

"Ida."
The mention of the name Ida instantly shot a spear through Frank's heart, and his stomach dropped. The girl immediately dragged Salian over to the swing set giggling,

and Salian - putting on an air of reluctance synonymous with how children always feel about the opposite sex - pushed her on the swing. Theatrically he rolled his eyes whenever one of the other boys looked over to them.

"Excuse me, sir. Can I help you?"

A young woman, presumably a teacher, curtly addressed Frank. She stood as tall as possible, with her arms folded. She ran a suspicious eye over the tall, middle-aged man, who was standing idly in a children's playground, sporting bloodstains which featured a shirt.

"Oh, yes! Good afternoon. Apologies for my appearance, young miss. My name is Frank Mossan."

He offered his hand to shake but the teacher's arms remained crossed. As she was ushering him back outside of the gates, she looked at him as though all he could offer was a bad smell.

"Ahem. I'm the head of security for the mall. Salian over there needed help returning to his mother, Ida, and said she worked here. Is that correct?"

The teacher's posture softened somewhat at the mention of Ida's name, but she still remained silent, investigative. Remembering that his security badge was in his blazer – which Salian was still cloaked in – he called over to the swing set.

"Salian! Could you bring me my-"

"Please don't address the children."

The teacher said, keeping a close eye on the man.

"I understand your concern, miss. And quite rightly too. But Salian came with me from the shopping centre. He got into some trouble there and I'm trying to return him to his mother. I'm not a ne'er-do-well or a vagrant, I promise. He's got my ID, if could just-"

Every time Frank tried to look over the teacher's shoulder towards Salian, the teacher parried his move and blocked his view.

"I'm sorry, sir. What was your name? Frank? Well, Frank, you seem courteous enough. However, given your appearance you must understand I cannot let you on school grounds. You are a stranger to me and the children and I will not compromise their safety in any way. Now, let us not make a scene, please. Kindly leave the premises and I shan't have to call the authorities to have you taken away."

Frank saw how seriously the teacher took her job, and he had a respect for her as a fellow protector. Her eyes; blue, steely, sincere, *had no time for nonsense*. The same theme followed in her fashion as she wore professional greys and whites, and her dark, sleek hair was scraped up in a tight bun. *Not one strand out of place, like she's going to read out the 6 o'clock news*. Frank gave her a nod.

"I understand, miss. Thank you for your patience... Please see that Salian- he's over there by the swings, pushing Polly – please see that his mother, Ida knows he's down here. He said she works upstairs. Anyway, I'll leave you to do your duties, miss. I appreciate the protection you're giving these children... Oh, just before I go, I'm investigating a missing girl. I wonder if she goes to this school, or if you have seen her at all?"

Frank produced the photo and placed his callused index finger to where the girl was in the shot. The teacher, not wanting to get close to this potentially unstable man, snatched it from him and examined the picture. She stared at it for a second, before muttering

"No, it can't be."

She adjusted her glasses which were at the end of her nose and pushed them as close to her eyes as she could. She squinted. She turned the photo to get more light on it. It went closer to her face, then further away, then closer again.

"Where did you get this photograph?"

"It was taken earlier today, miss. This was at the jewellery shop, in the shopping centre... Where I work."

"Wait here. Don't move a muscle! If you step foot on this playground, I'll call the police."

She backed away from Frank, never turning from him as she went towards the entrance of the building. Frank could still see the whites of her eyes staring at him when she reached the front door and spoke to somebody over the intercom. After she had finished speaking to whoever it was - *Charlie, maybe* - she remained by the front door of the building. Frank obeyed her wishes, he stayed outside of the playground. He could hear the children playing on the climbing frame, running around by the football goals, laughing and rolling in the grass, but he dared not look over to them in case the teacher took that as a reason to call the police. Instead, he remained looking over at the teacher, he gave her a toothless half-smile and did his best to appear harmless, *everyone's worried about nonces these days*. This act of intentional meekness in turn – as it always does – made him look like more of a criminal to the teacher, who's blue eyes were doing all they could to freeze him in place. Finally, the door opened. A woman exited. She was wearing a comfy looking oatmeal cardigan over a burnt-orange dress. Her hair was partly greying, and there was an obvious attempt to style it even though the unwieldy, thick, silver wires were *having none of it*. Her and the teacher spoke for a while, both of them looking over towards Frank. At that point, Frank had been trying so hard to look unimposing that all the effort had caused a flop sweat to appear, only increasing his conspicuousness, *well that's just bloody perfect isn't it, a sweaty pervert standing outside the school gates.* The knitwear-cloaked woman clearly thanked the teacher as she put a reassuring arm around her before walking over to the swing set. She picked Salian up and gave him a hug. After putting him back down she knelt in front of him and tenderly turned his face in both directions with her palms, checking for any meaningful damage behind his eyes. She hugged him again, removed Frank's blazer from his shoulders, kissed his forehead, and sent him over to stand next to the teacher who was still in the doorway, watching Frank. The woman marched towards Frank.

"Ida, I presume? Nice to meet you, I'm Fra-"
Once she got within proximity, she whipped the blazer towards Frank. It wrapped around his face and he immediately stopped talking. When he had unwrapped the navy-blue jacket from his head, the woman was uncomfortably close.

"Listen to me you creep. I don't know where you got this photo of me from but if I ever see you around my son again, I'll have you arrested. Do you understand?"
Frank went to confirm his comprehension of the woman's request with a snappy 'yes', but she didn't leave enough of a pause even for that. She went on reprimanding Frank as though he was one of Salian's bad-influence 'friends'.

"What do you think you're doing with a picture of a young girl like this anyway?"
The admonishment continued and Frank was totally perplexed. *It's her in the photo? How could that possibly be? How could that possibly be right?* The verbal tirade was in
209

full swing and as soon as he spotted an opening, Frank interjected with a question.

"This is you in the photo? But I've been looking for this little girl all day. How can that be?"

"Well, I'd say you're a little late on that mission." Ida scoffed, "This picture was taken a long time ago. I was lost in that horrible mall as a little girl and nobody came to find me. I had to find my own way out. Such a horrible memory. And just as I think I'd seen the back of it for good, a creepy old man comes wandering in waving this bloody picture around. Get out of here, you hear me? Sod off you creep."

Frank could see how distressed his presence made Ida.

"I'm leaving. I'm truly sorry to cause any upset. I really didn't mean to. You won't see me again ma'am, you have my word – whatever that's worth to you. Good evening miss."

He put his blazer on and began to walk away.

"Frank!"

He heard Salian shout out. Frank briefly looked over his shoulder and saw Salian waving at him. He wanted to wave back, but worried about the calamity which might ensue if he did. He gave a subtle nod to the boy, *definitely stuffed it*, and began to walk down the hill. In the distance, to the west of the high street he could see fields and trees, *might as well make the most of the sunset*, he headed towards them.

16

Frank couldn't wrap his head around it. How was Ida the woman in the photo? He had only ever seen the young girl in the picture. It was all he had to go off for the search. *Surely, she was mistaken, it can't be her in the photograph,* he thought. Then he recounted all the shop owners he had asked during the day. They had all claimed to see the girl, but at differing ages.

"And they were certain it was her."
He continued to mumble and mutter to himself as he walked down the hill, running the tips of his fingers over the coarse stone wall which segregated private rosebushes from public streetlamps. Most of the lights were off in the houses, and the few curtains that weren't quickly twitched and went dark as he passed.
But no-one can be certain of anything. If she was indeed the girl in the photo, the photo must have been taken prior to today... long before in fact. Frank thought about the way Artemis has metamorphosed over the course of the day, yet he still recognised her to be his beloved pet.
"Why didn't I have that same recognition with Ida then?"

Frank stopped talking to himself momentarily so he could smile at a dog walker who had *bitten off more than he could chew with that lot!* The dog walker, *sled more like*, was being pulled in Frank's direction. He hopped into the road for a moment to allow the dog walker – who was wrangling seven or eight dogs – keep all his clients' pets safe on the pavement. The dog walker mouthed the words 'thank you' to Frank as his arm was tugged along by eager leashes as he bumbled by. Soon after this courteous exchange, the dogs all began to bark incessantly at a cat who had hopped up onto one of the stone walls at a most unfortunate time, *eight left*. The ginger tabby shot off down the street, and the dogs – barking, panting, and drooling – gave chase after it, toppling over and dragging their walker behind them. Frank found the spectacle as humorous as it was violent. The dog walker had been dragged off as though he were a kite which refused to soar, bumping over the chipped asphalt, *dinging his frame and sail*. His hat was left behind and rolled back down the hill to Frank, a wide-brimmed, beige number, supposedly chosen because the walker had been expecting rain. Frank picked it up and, sure enough, some droplets began to hit his head.

     "Funny how things turn out."

He said, securing the hat to his head. As he lowered his arms again, he felt a shooting pain in his left, followed by a hot sensation. The blood was still pouring out, and Frank could no longer think clearly about the issue of the woman at the school and the girl in the photograph. He felt *a little off*, then he felt *woozy*, then he felt *a little dizzy*. After a while he finally accepted that he did not feel well at all. Despite this, he kept going down the hill. The gradient allowed him to keep some momentum, *it's the only thing keeping me upright,* and before he knew it, he was well clear of the high street and the tall building, and he was long past the semi-detached houses with immaculate rosebushes behind him. Right under Frank's nose, the quaint village path had morphed into a country road. He looked behind and all he could see was fields, green, yellow, some purple with heather, and some more were *great big carpets* of poppies. The same was true on either side of him, in fact, it was hard to believe there had been any buildings at all mere moments ago. In the distance, peeking out behind a sheer bit of rock which the road was forced to curve around, he could see the stream which ran through the town. He carried on towards it, *it's flowing out to the sea, dispersing amongst the fish and sea life, joining the current and travelling for miles, then eventually it will come back inland, only to tour round, have more pigeons bathe in it, have more ice cream eating idiots marvel at it, and it will do this over and over...*

The stream shimmered intensely, *almost too much, that.* The sun had begun its descent behind the rolling fields and snaking roads. Frank's face screwed, his eyes squinted, and he raised his good arm to shade himself. Even with his peachy back-lit palm blocking the sun's light, the reflections in the ripples of the stream danced around his face, and he blinked sporadically.

"Can't see a damn thing with this sun in my eyes." His good arm felt much lighter than before, while the other was much, *much heavier, like it's a whole other person.* He recalled how fulfilling it felt to carry Salian on his back. He began to feel hollow, his stomach felt empty, but his mind had not translated this into hunger. Just a hollowed-out feeling. His legs imitated the weight of his still-draining arm

213

and he let gravity guide him and his limbs down the rest of the hill.

The sun had all but set by the time Frank had *schlepped* down to the river. Some wispy clouds had appeared, *thank God!* And they dispersed the direct light into oranges and pinks which bounced off the rippling brown water and murky green algae, *carrying silt all the same.* Even with this, *Bob Ross backdrop,* the reflection of the sun in the river was still too much for Frank, it seemed exhausting, his breath was short, and his soul ached. Practically blinded, he bumped into a small wooden sign which telegraphed the imminent fork in the path. Pointing straight ahead, a wooden arrow on the sign read:

TOWN CENTRE, HIGH STREET, AND RESIDENTIAL AREAS

The other sign, which pointed to the path which coiled left read:

HERMIT'S FOREST

The left path led Frank to a small wooden bridge covered with unfinished metal sheets – which were razor sharp at the corners, *health and safety nightmare, that* – held together by thick ropes which wrapped around the ends of the sheets, ensuring they did not bow under Frank's footsteps, and only swayed a little when he crossed. As he reached the end of the rickety death-trap, his foot slipped, *bloody shabby shoes!* And he clumsily stumbled off the bridge. He knocked into a piece of upright sheet metal which was acting as a post, and it found its jagged little way into his already gaping wound. He only stopped himself falling because his exposed bone was pressing against the serrated metal. With a great squeal, *like a pig at the abattoir*, he removed himself from the pole. His scream would have presumably echoed across the field had it not been for the dense, gloomy forest which sprawled out ahead of him. It soaked the squeal up, bouncing it from trunk to trunk, branch to branch, leaf to leaf, until the sound had no direction and fell dead on the forest floor. *An eerie silence, but a calm one, nonetheless.* The trees performed the same noise cancellation to the traffic from the road, the crowds outside the pubs, the dogs barking in the gardens, none of it made it past the first row of trees, the frontline defence from the clatter and the noise, all the grinding and screeching. Once Frank had taken just a few steps into the forest he couldn't hear anything except for the workings of his organs, he found it *grotesque*. He forgot about the outside world entirely and it was as if only he and the trees existed. The trees were leering and looming, and they were all he could see. However, Frank was not concerned about getting lost, Frank was leaving a slick red trail behind him which pooled up in the drag marks his shoes were creating, *not exactly breadcrumbs, but it'll do*. All this was going on behind Frank, but in front of him a clearing had appeared. He shuffled into the centre of the dusty circular mound and looked at the trees that reached up and connected their branches above his head, creating a perfect dome within the canopy. He looked down at the dirt and imagined a similar dome being formed by the roots which probably sprawled out underneath the earth, *as above*... Feeling left out, he removed his shoes and placed his bare feet on the dry uneven soil, he felt a welcome sensation. Throwing his jacket over a nearby log, Frank began the awkward business of removing his

215

gouged arm from his blood drenched sleeve. It clung to him like a second skin, and the white button-down had to be ripped further for him to successfully be freed from it. The shirt flew across the tree-dome and slapped onto the now well-dressed log. His great gaping wound was revealed, along with Frank's moles and freckles, Frank's inelegant body hair, and Frank's oily skin which had pushed deposits of salt into the creases left by his shirt to form little pale veins up and down his clammy torso. The effort of taking off the shirt had used up the last of his energy, he was grey and shivering. His voice turned raspy, and his breathing rattled. He dropped to all fours amongst the moss and roots and crocuses, and his eyelids felt heavy.

Tired. So damn tired.

From all fours he rolled onto one side, his eyes looked around for a while at the *barky womb,* but soon they began to close. They closed and opened at slower and slower intervals, synchronising with the frequency of his breathing, which were *the last gulps of a beached whale.* As he lay in the foetal position, the world grew dark. He remembered the pool bars of his youth; he remembered the stale smell of beer that wafted around in them. He remembered a certain perfume which at long last had cut through the stink, a floral fragrance with bitter notes. It was hers; it was always hers. 'Sarah' he mouthed.

He felt her hand on his shoulder take away the pain and he stopped shivering; the hand turned him onto his back. In the cage of branches winding and weaving overhead he saw feathered creatures of all sizes shuffling around, vying for a good spot to spectate the strange animal which was laying beneath them. Frank chuckled, which soon *metamorphosed* into a cough – there was blood in it. He exhaled; he looked

216

up again, past the branches, past the birds, past the leaves. It was still there, forever staring back at him with cold indifference. He inhaled; he felt the pressure of the moon crush down on him once more, only this time it didn't bother him. His eyes closed slowly, and the moon was gone. He exhaled once more, and the forest was gone. With his eyes closed and his body shutting down, all he could feel was the sensation of a river taking him out to sea. His body went limp and once again Frank fell asleep.

For the quietest time, for the longest time, for the last time.

EPILOGUE

"Honey, wake up. You're going to be late again."
In a pool of sweat, Salian sat bolt upright in the bed next to his wife.

"What time is it?"
Before his partner could answer, Salian picked up the alarm clock sitting on his bedside table and squinted at it.

"Shit, Fi. It's five to eight!"

"I tried to wake you earlier, but you were still as a rock. Do you want coffee? I'll get up with you and make you one."

"No time, Fi. You stay in bed, no use both of us being miserable. Anyway, you should rest, you've got the exam later... Yeah, I can't wait to find out, can you? Are there any clean shirts? This one smells like smoke."

"Yes, I hung some up over the towel rail in the bathroom... Don't hurt yourself rushing around like that! Really?...They're still a bit damp!? Well, I'm sure it'll dry a bit once you put it on. Be careful running down the stairs for god's sake! What were you- yeah, there's one left in the bread bin I think... What were you dreaming about anyway?"

Salian hopped back into the bedroom to answer Fiona, but before he did, he put his other leg into his trousers and removed the croissant from his mouth, chewing on a mouthful of it.

"You remember I told you about when I was in the old mall the day it collapsed?"

"Yeah. Reliving that again, were you? Ooh, must've been hectic!"

"You'd think so, but it was quite a pleasant dream actually. I saw Frank again, the security guard... What? Is he the one who what?! No, God, no! That's just something my mum said about him, because she was upset when she met him. He wouldn't hurt a fly... Because I just know, ok? I know he was a good man, please don't speak like that about him." Salian sat on a rickety chair in the corner of the pokey bedroom attempting to simultaneously tie his shoelaces, eat his breakfast, and correct parts of the story which Fiona had been told by Ida on one of their weekly brunches.

"Anyway, all the shit I saw that day would have been enough for me to see my therapist about regardless, right? Yeah, well, on top of all that... What? Oh, I dunno. They reckon around ten more sessions... Yeah, well no-one's ever fully cured are they - I think it's more like they've helped all they can with me... What would be the point? I'd have to tell a whole new therapist my life story again, fuck that. What? No, we've been through this, I don't want to be stuck on medication for the rest of my life... Yeah, well it's up and down innit. Fi, will you let me finish my story? Honestly, how can someone so tired have so many questions in them. Right, so anyway. On top of all the events that day, guess who gets reported as missing about a month after? That's right, Frank does. Some hikers found his jacket with his name badge and some other clothing with blood samples in the forest... No, never found him. The guys who were working that case had to presume his body got taken out by the river. Yeah, I was looking at the old case file yesterday at the office."

Fiona laid on her side and curled up to keep herself warm.

"Well, no wonder you dreamt about him them. Don't get too obsessed with it, Sal. You know how you get. It won't do you any good."

"Yeah, I know. Right, I'm off... Have you seen my name badge? The lads at the station won't let me live it down if I forget it again... Oh shit, there it is."

Salian removed the name badge from his trouser pocket and affixed it to the lapel of his jacket.

"I love you."

Fiona said as Salian hastily went out the door. He shouted back to her.

"You too."

Fiona laid in bed and finished the *perfectly good* croissant Salian had *wasted*. She reached over to the bedside table and read the appointment card.

We look forward to seeing you at your next appointment. Please ensure that you arrive in plenty of time for your appointment to ensure you can park. We also ask that you arrive 10 minutes prior to the appointment time stated on your letter so that you may have routine observations performed and recorded prior to having your scan/seeing the Doctor.

On arrival, please report to the reception area - *yaddah yaddah yaddah* - Please ensure you bring your Pregnancy Care Record to every appointment - *Blah Blah Blah, ah here we go, scans.* - During your pregnancy you will normally be offered two scans. The first scan will ideally be around 12 weeks to date your pregnancy and offer screening for Downs/Edwards/Patau Syndrome. The second scan at 18-21 weeks is carried out to check your baby is developing as expected. However, it is important to realise that not all developmental concerns can be identified on an ultrasound scan. Further scans will not be routinely offered.

When attending for your first scan appointment, at around 12 weeks of pregnancy, please ensure that you have a full bladder, by drinking plenty of water before you atte-*oh shit.*

Fiona's left foot was the first appendage brave enough to exit the warmth of the duvet, followed by her right. She went downstairs to fix herself a glass of water and to *put the kettle on... just to be sure.* She sat at the kitchen table and finished the last bite of the last croissant of the pack. She sipped at her water to remove the *claggy, buttery feel* in her mouth. She swirled some water around her mouth and smacked her lips together. Out loud to the empty kitchen she said.

"Frankie."

She liked the sound of it so much that she said it again.

"Frankie... Boy or girl, Frankie's a nice name."

END

Printed in Great Britain
by Amazon

36044501R00128